The Collected Th

Thraxas Book Eleven

Thraxas of Turai

Martin Scott

Thraxas of Turai

Thraxas of Turai is the eleventh book in the series. Thraxas, perhaps the doughtiest warrior ever born within that city's walls, (as he describes himself) is almost home. The army led by Lisutaris reaches Turai, ready to retake their city. Thraxas begins the book in some trouble, having been flung in the stockade following a disreputable brawl, but will soon be back in action, investigating a politically awkward murder while making ready for battle. At his side is Makri, whose mathematical skills are called upon for some complicated sorcerous calculations designed to bring down the walls. There are dragons in the sky, hostile forces ahead, and, worst of all as far as Thraxas is concerned, a general beer shortage. When this is all over, Thraxas intends to spend the rest of his days sitting comfortably in his favourite tavern. But first, he has a city to retake.

For more about Thraxas visit
www.thraxas.com
www.martinmillar.com

Cover Model: Madeline Rae Mason

Thraxas of Turai
Copyright © Martin Millar 2019

This edition published 2019 by Martin Millar

The moral right of the author has been asserted. All rights reserved. No part of this book may be reproduced or transmitted in any form or by any means without written permission from the copyright holder.

All characters in the publication are fictitious, and any resemblance to real persons, living or dead, is purely coincidental.

ISBN 978-1792849992

Introduction to Thraxas Book Eleven

Thraxas of Turai has taken me longer to write than I intended. I'm not certain why. I've been keen for Thraxas to return home to Turai for a long time, but writing the book was a slow process. It was frustrating. There were periods where I hardly seemed able to make any progress at all. I can't explain why that was. When I write the next Thraxas book, I'm sure I'll be able to do it more quickly.

Still, Thraxas has finally arrived at the walls of Turai. Accompanied by Makri, in an army led by Lisutaris, all he has to accomplish now is the retaking the city from the occupying forces. Then he might be able to settle down again in his home, his favourite tavern, the Avenging Axe, in front of a roaring fire with a flagon of ale close at hand. Thraxas has not enjoyed his period of exile. As a young man he did travel the world, but these days he's a dedicated city-dweller, no longer suited to roaming around. Like Thraxas, Lisutaris's only ambition is to rest. Makri, on the other hand, is still full of ambition, and has not given up on her dreams.

Martin Millar

Thraxas of Turai

Chapter One

As an army on the march, the combined forces of the west don't have access to prison cells. They do have a portable stockade for the temporary confinement of soldiers who've stepped out of line. It's basic but effective. The wooden walls are only two meters tall but the whole edifice is protected by a spell that makes it impossible to escape. Once you're thrown in the stockade there's not much to do but sit on the ground and wait till you're released. If the weather is too cold or too hot, that's unfortunate. Emergency field imprisonment doesn't come with any blankets. I know this as I'm currently sitting in the stockade with a sore head, watching the last of the moons disappear from view behind the walls and the first rays of dawn appear in the sky.

It goes without saying that I should not be here. Thraxas of Turai, perhaps the doughtiest warrior ever born within that city's walls, does not deserve to be flung in the stockade. The entire episode is just one more in the long line of indignities thrust upon me by a city whose rulers have always done their utmost to hinder, belittle, and hold me back in every way possible. When I see our War Leader, I'll have something to say about it.

I clamber to my feet. 'Wait till I see Lisutaris!' I roar. 'I'll have something to say about this.'

'Quieten down in there,' shouts a guard, from outside.

'Let me out of here immediately!'

There's no reply. I try again. 'I demand my legal rights! Release me from this confinement, you dogs!' Again there's no reply. I shake my head in frustration. There are three other soldiers here, plus a Simnian chef and a junior sorcerer lying in the corner, his rainbow cloak torn and mud-stained from whatever dishonourable affair he's been involved in. A young lad in a Samsarinan private's uniform sitting with his back to the fence yawns, then looks up at me. 'What are you in here for?'

'For reasons of grave injustice! The fate of all honest men under these despots who seek to crush the common man with unjust allegations and wilful assaults on their rights and dignity.'

'What did you actually do?'

'I've no idea,' I admit. 'Last thing I remember I was playing cards and drinking beer.'

'You probably got drunk and started a fight.'

I give the young Samsarinan a withering look and do not deign to reply. Thraxas of Turai does not get drunk and start fights. Particularly since he became Chief Security Officer to Lisutaris, Mistress of the Sky, Commander and War Leader of the forces of the west, currently marching east to confront Prince Amrag and his Orcish horde. Two weeks ago we inflicted a crushing defeat on his advancing forces, the greatest success any Human army has ever recorded against the Orcish Prince. Up till then he'd beaten us in every engagement. That came to an end when Lisutaris, destroyed his troops near the Simnian border. Since then we've marched east towards Turai, ready to chase the Orcs back to where they belong. Our soldiers, previously demoralised by Prince Amrag's invincibility, have taken heart and now approach battle with confidence. All of which makes it more inexplicable that the army has chosen to throw me in the stockade. At a time like this our best men should be on active service, not languishing in some hellish temporary prison.

The wooden door is hauled open. In walks Hanama; probably the last person I'd want to see at this moment. Hanama used to be third in command of the Turanian Assassins Guild. Now, in an inexplicable lapse of judgement, Lisutaris has recruited her into the Sorcerers Auxiliary Regiment, made her a captain, and appointed her head of her personal intelligence unit. Accompanying Hanama is a Samsarinan sergeant. He asks Hanama who she's looking for.

'The drunken idiot,' she mutters.

I draw myself up. 'Are you referring to me? I'd advise you to change your tone, Captain Hanama. Captain Thraxas does not appreciate–' A sudden flash of pain in my head brings me to a halt.

While I won't allow anyone to call me a drunken idiot, my headache and current fragile state of health do indicate some consumption of alcohol last night.

Hanama's a small, dark-haired woman. She's pale-skinned to an unhealthy degree, like a woman who never goes out in sunlight. Not surprising, I suppose. Back in Turai she'd generally be cloaked and hooded; here she wears the standard military uniform of the intelligence branch of the Sorcerers Auxiliary Regiment, mainly black, with the addition of a non-regulation black cloth headpiece which covers her forehead, ears and neck. She's wearing a loose scarf, pulled up to cover the lower part of her face so that not much more than her eyes are visible. Not a sight you'd want to wake up to after a night spent on rough ground. She produces a small sheet of paper and shows it to the sergeant. He nods, then motions to the private by the gate to bring him a quill pen. He signs my release then ushers us out the door. The door shuts. I glare at Hanama. 'Why did they send you?' She doesn't reply, but walks on. I hurry after her. 'Couldn't Makri have got me out?'

'Ensign Makri is busy doing her job as bodyguard to our War Leader.'

We pass through the pitched tents of the Simnian infantry. The camp is coming to life as soldiers emerge from their tents to cook breakfast.

'I'm sure other people were available. Some loyal member of my security unit, for instance. Or Gurd. Did you bring me a lesada leaf?'

'Why would I do that?'

'Standard procedure for comrades rescuing another comrade after a night in the stockade. Banishes any slight trace of hangover that may have occurred.'

'I didn't bring you a leaf.'

'Gurd would have. Of all the people Lisutaris could have sent to get me out of jail you're the last person she should have picked.'

Hanama halts. She turns to towards me. 'Captain Thraxas, I'd have happily let you rot in the stockade for the rest of your days. The last thing I want to be wasting my time on is freeing you from the results of your drunken stupidity. However, as that drunken stupidity appears to have involved Commander Lisutaris in a difficult situation, I was deemed the most appropriate person to escort you to our War Leader's tent.'

I'm finding this hard to take in. 'What happened?'

'Don't you remember any of it?'

'No.'

'Then you really should drink less.'

And with that, Captain Hanama falls silent. I follow her back through the camp, heading for the Lisutaris's command post, wondering what the hell happened last night. I can't remember a thing. Friendly game of cards and a few beers, as far as I was concerned.

Chapter Two

Our army is encamped close to the eastern border of Simnia. We're not far from Turai, our destination. To reach there we'll have to pass through the northern part of Attical, a small nation that, like Turai, is a member of the League of City States. At one time these states would have come to each other's assistance but those days have passed. When Turai fell to the Orcs, the citizens of Attical withdrew into their city and barred the gates, as did every other member of the League. I don't blame them. Had the situation been reversed, Turai wouldn't have helped them either.

Months after the fall of Turai, the larger nations of the West - Simnia, Nioj, Samsarina - along with an Elvish army from the south, have finally gathered their forces to march back east. What we'll find when we get there, we still don't know. As far as I'm aware, no reliable scouting reports from Turai have yet come back to us. The Orcs will be firmly embedded in the captured city by now. Their sorcery will have blanketed the area. Gathering information won't be easy. As our intelligence unit is headed by Captain Hanama, I have no confidence in their abilities.

Hanama marches a few steps in front of me, giving every impression of a woman who'd rather not be seen in my company. Not that anyone pays much attention to us. Everyone is used to soldiers from foreign lands wandering through their ranks. The Simnians don't pay much heed to the sight of two Turanian captains, one smart, one bedraggled, strolling through their midst; they're more intent of cooking breakfast. We've been camped here for several days and no one knows when we'll be advancing. As we pass into the area occupied by the Sorcerers Auxiliary Regiment I recognise a few more familiar faces. Gurd, for one, who laughs as I come into view, and nudges the soldier next to him, who also laughs. The entire regiment will be aware that I spent the night in the stockade. Gurd, my old fighting companion, has spent a few nights there too in his time. Beyond the encampment of the Auxiliary Regiment stands Lisutaris's command centre, a large square tent, more solid looking than most though just as frayed and weather-beaten as the others after our long march. Not far from the command centre is a wagon and several tents belonging to Lisutaris's personal security unit, under my command.

'Well, thanks for bailing me out,' I say to Hanama. 'Time for me to get back to work.'

'Commander Lisutaris wants to see you immediately.'

'I should probably tidy up a little—'

'Her instructions were to bring you directly, with no delay.'

I sigh, and follow along. 'Can't a man have a few drinks and a quiet game of cards without being lectured by our War Leader? You'd think she'd have better things to do. Plans to make. You really can't see any reason for her to get involved in a minor affair like this.'

Hanama doesn't reply. She's never been a talkative woman. Although she is rather well-spoken. She has a soft voice, never uses slang, and generally sounds educated. I've no idea where she might have been educated. I've encountered her often but I know very little about her background. At some point in her life she transformed from a small schoolgirl into a small, deadly assassin, but I couldn't even guess how that happened. The guards at Lisutaris's tent acknowledge her as we pass. Inside we find Lisutaris, in her dark blue cloak with its discrete rainbow sorcerer's motif, studying maps with the aid of a tiny sorcerous light which floats above her shoulder. Makri is lurking behind her. I frown. I have the feeling I'm about to be lectured about excessive drinking by three women, not something a warrior like myself should have to suffer. It would never have happened in the old days. Commander Lisutaris asks Captain Hanama if I'm sober.

'I don't know. I can't tell.'

'Yes, I'm sober. Thanks for getting me out of the stockade, Commander. I really should be getting back to my unit.'

Lisutaris, Mistress of the Sky, is a few years younger than me. She's a lot better preserved. She was a rich woman, back in Turai. She's Head of the Sorcerers Guild, and the most powerful sorcerer in the west. There were some objections to her appointment as War Leader but her victory over Prince Amrag put an end to any discontent. Her authority is now undisputed. That makes the way she's glaring at me uncomfortable. Hostile, as far as I can judge. I wonder if I should remind her of the many times I've come to her assistance. She'd have died in Turai if I hadn't dragged her out of the burning city. Makri too, not that she's ever been grateful for the rescue.

'Captain Thraxas, do you know anything about the death of the Niojan, Captain Istaros?'

'He's dead?'

'Yes. And you were playing cards with him last night.'

'I have a few gaps in my memory. What happened?'

'I was hoping you could enlighten me. His body was found not far from General Maldon's tent.'

'He was still healthy when they dragged me off to the stockade.'

'Nothing happened during the card game that could give you a hint as to why he might have been murdered?'

'Nothing.'

'Not surprising, I suppose,' says Lisutaris. 'You were reportedly in no state to register anything. Do you know a man called Magranos?'

'You mean chief steward to Baron Vosanos?'

'In civilian life, yes. He's now a major in the Samsarinan army. Or was.'

'Is he dead too?'

'Yes. Violently killed, without witnesses as far as we can learn. His body was found not far from that of Captain Istaros.'

'He wasn't at the card game. I'd remember.'

'I doubt you would. But no, he wasn't at the card game. However he was murdered nearby, around the same time.' Our War leader glares at me. 'So we have one Samsarinan Major and one Niojan Captain murdered after a card game at a Simnian General's tent. You were there. As my head of security, one might hope you could shed light on the affair. Even solve the mystery quickly, thereby saving me from aggravation. But you can't, can you?'

I remain silent.

'Because instead of maintaining the alert manner I might expect from my head of security, you decided to get drunk, accuse a Simnian major of cheating and start a brawl which resulted in the guards dragging you off to the stockade.' Lisutaris scowls at me. 'Didn't I specifically instruct you not to drink to excess?'

'Yes, Commander.'

Behind Lisutaris, Makri is looking on smugly. Makri, or Ensign Makri as she now is, has been doing her best to be a professional soldier ever since Lisutaris recruited her as her bodyguard. It's not the first time she's shown disapproval at some supposed lack of professionalism on my part, a staggeringly hypocritical stance from an ex-gladiator with Orcish blood who hardly knew what civilisation meant till I instructed her on the finer points of Turanian culture. She washed up in the city after slaughtering her Orcish Lord and his entourage and fleeing here from the east, and it's fair to say she'd never have got anywhere without me looking after her every step of the way.

'Captain Thraxas. Find out what happened and sort it out quickly. I'm too busy to be distracted and I won't have my armies unsettled while we're on the verge of confronting the Orcs.'

'Two murders are not necessarily going to be easy to sort out quickly.'

'They had better be. If I didn't need you to do this you'd still be in the stockade. As it is I'll let you off with a fine of one weeks wages.'

'That seems very–'

I'm interrupted by the arrival of Captain Julius, our War Leader's young aide-de-camp. He enters the tent, salutes smartly, and informs Lisutaris that Sareepa is waiting outside.

'Very good,' replies Lisutaris. 'Bring her in as soon as Captain Thraxas leaves.'

Lisutaris tells me I can go. Suddenly I'm not as keen to leave. 'Did he just say *Sareepa*?'

'Yes.'

'Sareepa Lightning Strikes the Mountain? Head of the Mattesh Sorcerers Guild?'

'Yes.'

'What's she doing here?'

'She's come to help the war effort, of course.'

I wasn't expecting this. Mattesh, a small city-state, is Turai's southern neighbour. I'd have thought every Matteshan sorcerer would be holed up in their city. Presumably Lisutaris has ordered them here, to boost our attack. It's understandable. We're gambling everything on our attack being successful. If we lose, Mattesh will fall soon enough, no matter where their sorcerers are.

'Does this tent have a back door?'

Lisutaris glares at me. 'A back door? What is this nonsense?'

'I'm not that keen on meeting Sareepa.'

'Why on earth not?'

'There was... some awkwardness at the Sorcerers Assemblage.'

Makri is unable to prevent herself from laughing. She cuts it off quickly and looks embarrassed. Lisutaris glares at her, then back at me. Since she became War leader, Lisutaris has done a lot of glaring. 'I'm fighting a war, Captain Thraxas. Whatever oafish behaviour you were involved in at the Sorcerers Assemblage is no concern of mine.'

'Well, really, it wasn't my–'

'Dismissed, Captain Thraxas.'

I trudge out of the command tent. There, at the head of six Matteshan sorcerers, stands Sareepa Lightning Strikes the Mountain. She's a strong, well-built woman. As soon as she sees me, she narrows her eyes.

'Thraxas.'

'Sareepa.'

She glances at my uniform. 'They made you a captain? Now I know we're going to lose. We should have stayed in Mattesh.'

'Pleasure to meet you again,' I mumble, and hurry off. I can feel Sareepa's eyes following me as I depart. Just as well I wear such a good spell protection charm. Sareepa's a powerful sorcerer; not the sort of person you want to offend.

'Too late for that,' I reflect, pausing when I'm a safe distance away. So far it's been a very poor morning. I wake up with a hangover in a stockade, I'm fined a week's wages, and a powerful sorcerer who bears me a grudge has just arrived in camp. I shake my head at the injustice of it all. From Lisutaris's abrupt manner and unnecessary punishment you'd never guess I'd saved her life on more than one occasion. I trudge the short distance to my wagon, beside which are two horses, in good condition, and three tents, badly weather-beaten but holding together due to the competent sorcery of Anumaris Thunderbolt and Rinderan, both members of my security unit. Neither is in sight as I arrive but the third member of my staff is. Sendroo-ir-Vallis, commonly known as Droo, a young Elf temporarily seconded to the Sorcerers Auxiliary Regiment. She takes one look at me and bursts out laughing.

'I heard they flung you in the stockade!' Droo has apparently never come across anything so amusing and has to support herself by leaning on the wagon as her laughter threatens to overwhelm her small frame.

'Could you reign in the laughter and do something useful? I need a–'

Droo holds out a fistful of lesada leaves, having anticipated my need. The first time I met Sendroo was on the Elvish Isle of Avula where she spent her time writing poetry, drinking wine, and falling out of trees. I wouldn't say she was the greatest asset to my unit in terms of security experience but she does know about some of the important things in life. I take a leaf, cram it in my mouth, and chew. The lesada leaf is the greatest hangover cure in existence, an almost magical substance grown only in the Elvish Isles. They can be hard to get hold of unless you have Elvish contacts. I clamber into the wagon and sit down. Droo hops in after me.

'What happened?'

'Not got the clearest of recollections,' I admit. 'I vaguely remember some Simnian dog was cheating and I was obliged to confront him. After that, things got out of hand.' As the lesada leaf takes effect, my head begins to clear. 'Where are Anumaris and Rinderan?'

Droo doesn't know. 'I had to report to Captain Ir-Mesnith this morning. When I got back they were gone.'

Droo came to the mainland as part of the Elvish army. Though she's been seconded to my unit she's expected to liaise with the Elves every few days. Lisutaris sees this as good for co-operation between Humans and Elves. I was inclined to see it as the Elves poking their noses into my private business until Droo began appearing back from their meetings with flagons of good quality Elvish wine, after which I saw it as not such a bad thing. I've instructed her to tell them nothing and keep bringing back the wine.

'Did you win at cards?'

I shake my head. 'Not one of my finest nights. Now I'm broke. Wouldn't be so bad if Lisutaris hadn't fined me a weeks wages. The woman is a tyrant.'

'Don't you have money in reserve?'

It's true, I do. In Samsarina I masterminded a stupendous gambling campaign when Makri won the swordfighting tournament. I ended up winning over ten thousand gurans. 'It's all stored away in Lisutaris's magic pocket. That makes it awkward to ask for it right now. Wouldn't surprise me if she's already spent it.'

'I'm sure our Commander wouldn't steal your money.'

'Who knows what's she's been doing? The woman is crazed with power. Nothing would surprise me.' I drink some of Droo's wine. 'Did the Elves have any idea when we're advancing?'

'No one knows why we're waiting.'

The canvas at the back of the wagon opens and Anumaris appears. Anumaris Thunderbolt, Storm Class Sorcerer, is neat and tidy, more so than you'd expect after weeks on the march, her grey cloak spotless and the sorcerer's rainbow insignia clearly visible at her shoulder. In most ways she's an excellent asset to my unit. She's intelligent, conscientious, efficient, brave, and quite powerful for such a young sorcerer. Unfortunately she has a tendency to disapprove of the normal relaxations of the hard-working soldier, namely beer.

'Captain Thraxas,' she says, rather stiffly.

'If you're about to launch into one of your lectures on the evils of drinking, forget it. And don't bother running off to tell our War Leader either.' Lisutaris specifically instructed the young sorcerer to discourage me from drinking. It's an affront to my dignity and a tremendous hindrance to the war effort, but I seem to be stuck with it.

'I was not about to launch into a lecture.' Anumaris climbs into the wagon. 'I'm just here to report on my intelligence gathering.'

'Learned anything interesting?'

'The Simnian fourth cavalry are threatening to sue the Turanian high command for damage to their property. They claim you wrecked three tents and a wagon, destroyed a stove and were responsible for injuries to five Simnian soldiers. The Simnian commander has promised to raise the matter with our Commander.'

I wave this aside. 'Just goes to show what a weak, useless bunch the Simnians are. Who makes a fuss over a little brawl in wartime?'

'This doesn't reflect very well on me, Captain! Our Commander instructed you to stay sober and entrusted me with ensuring you did!'

I'm about to make a furious retort but I reel it in. Anumaris has been doing a good job in my unit. Much as I resent her spying on me, it's not her fault. Lisutaris did see fit to issue specific instructions over my beer intake. 'Forget it, Anumaris. Lisutaris won't hold it against you. She's known me for a long time and she doesn't expect you to put me on the straight and narrow. It's already cost me a week's wages, I'll make sure there are no more repercussions.'

'There may be. The Simnians are furious.'

'Anumaris. About seventeen years ago I stood beside Lisutaris, defending the walls of Turai. There were dragons in the sky and squadrons of Orcs swarming up ladders. We were right next to each other when the wall collapsed. With history like that, she's not going to throw me to the wolves just because a bunch of Simnians are upset.'

The young sorcerer doesn't look convinced. 'You were standing together on the walls?'

'Yes. Lisutaris had been assigned to protect the section my unit was defending. By the end of the day we were the only two people left standing. I was using a spear to keep the Orcs back, and when Lisutaris ran out of spells she picked up a broken sword and joined in. A wounded dragon crashed into the wall and brought it down, which would have been the end for Turai if the Elvish army hadn't turned up at the last moment. It was a miracle we survived, but we did.'

Surprisingly, this is all true. It's one of the few stories I don't need to exaggerate. 'Lisutaris isn't going to come down too hard on one of the only Turanians she can trust in a crisis.'

I ask Anumaris if she and Rinderan picked up anything on their morning scan. It's part of their duties to examine the area around our War Leader for any possible sorcerous intrusion. Deeziz the Unseen and the Orcish sorcerers have caused us problems recently but our own sorcerers are prepared for them now.

'I left Ensign Rinderan to do the scans,' says Anumaris. 'While I investigated the murders. At the card game you were at. Before–'

'Before I got hauled off. Why were you investigating them?'

'I knew you'd be asked to. I thought it would be wise to make some enquiries while events were still fresh in people's minds.'

'Good initiative. Did you learn anything?'

Before Anumaris can reply, the colour drains from her cheeks and she sways on her feet. She sits down rapidly and for a moment looks as if she's about to pass out.

'What's the matter?'

The young sorcerer takes some deep breaths. 'Sorry Captain. I used a spell earlier, it must have taken more out of me than I realised. I'm feeling better now. What was I saying?'

'You were telling me about your investigation. What's this about a spell?'

'I'll get to that in a moment,' says Anumaris. 'I went to both places the bodies were found. Captain Istaros was lying behind his own tent. He'd been stabbed. It looked like he'd been attacked from behind and killed without a struggle. Major Magranos was killed not far away.'

'You mean he was in the Niojan encampment too?'

'Yes, near their perimeter. No one seemed to know why he'd have been there. It looked like he'd put up more of a fight. He had some defensive wounds and he'd been facing his opponent when he was killed. It can't have been a long fight because no one heard anything. I didn't learn much from my observations because soldiers from the Niojan security units were there and they'd trampled over everything.' Anumaris pauses, taking another deep breath. 'I did find this.' She holds out a small brass badge. I don't recognise which unit or even which army it's from.

'It was trampled into the grass beside Captain Istaros's tent,' continues Anumaris. 'I only found it because I used a spell for locating items that had recently been brought into the area.'

I'm impressed. 'That's an advanced spell.'

'I used it twice. I didn't realise how much it would take out of me.'

I study the small metal badge. 'Good work, Anumaris. Did you find anything similar near Major Magranos?'

'No. But my spell was weaker the second time.' Anumaris has regained her strength. She climbs to her feet. 'I did find out something interesting. Captain Istaros was a nephew of King Lamachus.'

King Lamachus is the ruler of Nioj and that's a nation our Commander won't want to offend. They're powerful and they've never been friendly towards Turai.

'That's unfortunate. Lisutaris wants this all dealt with quickly without any upsets. Difficult to do that with the King's nephew involved.'

'Difficult to sweep it under the bushes, you mean,' says Droo.

'Exactly.'

Anumaris looks puzzled. 'What do you mean, *sweep it under bushes?*'

'I mean make it go away without causing any fuss.'

'How could we do that? There's bound to be a fuss after two murders.'

'In normal circumstances, yes. Here, maybe not. We're about to fight the most important battle in our history. Lisutaris doesn't want any distractions.'

The young sorcerer is dissatisfied. 'This rather sounds like you'd consider letting someone off with murder if it was convenient.'

'That's exactly what I meant.'

'But that's not right.'

'It's right if it keeps the army focused. Possibly it won't come to that. I'll have a better idea of what's going on after you've taken me to the crime scenes. Which you can do right after I've had breakfast.' At that moment there's a tremendous noise outside as every trumpeter in the army starts playing a familiar refrain. Anumaris Thunderbolt leaps to her feet. 'They're sounding the advance!'

So much for visiting the crime scenes. I peer out the back of the wagon. Already clouds of dust are billowing into the air as battalions form up and regiments prepare to march. There's a lot of noise as soldiers bolt down the last of their breakfasts, strapping on their armour while running into formation. Horses wheel around, light troops sprint towards their marching positions at the front and the heavy phalanxes raise their spears as they stride forward. Anumaris is already outside, casting the spell which will move our tents quickly into their bags. Rinderan appears at a run and starts using his own sorcery to toss all our equipment into the wagon. Droo is attaching the horses. When they're in place she leaps onto the pillion and grabs the reigns.

'We're ready to go, Captain Thraxas.'

I glare at them all. 'Dammit. Couldn't they have waited till I'd had breakfast?'

Chapter Three

We advance steadily till the early afternoon when the trumpets sound, calling a halt. If we're following standard practice we should have about an hour before we move on again. My wagon is not far behind Lisutaris's entourage and as we come to a halt I stand on the pillion, squinting against the bright sun, wondering if Makri might be in view. She usually remains close to Lisutaris, but our War Leader does exclude her from the most secret meetings with her army chiefs. I spot her right away, distinctive in her light Orcish armour with her long hair hanging down her back. I instruct my unit not to eat all the food while I'm gone then hurry through the ranks of the Sorcerers Auxiliary Regiment.

'Banished from a secret meeting again?'

Makri grunts. She doesn't like it when this happens, feeling that her job is to be close to Lisutaris at all times.

'I need to talk to you anyway. I could do with your opinion.'

Makri is a little shorter than me. She's strong and lithe, with a sword at each hip. One is a bright Elvish blade, a beautiful weapon from the Isle of Avula. The other is a black Orcish sword, brought with her from the east. No-one one else in our army carries such a weapon. Most people wouldn't even go near it. Makri keeps it sheathed as even the sight of it would cause offence to the Elves. Her light Orcish armour, leather and chainmail, makes her stand out, though she stands out anyway, with her reddish skin. It's struck me before that it's perverse of Makri to insist on wearing the Orcish armour and carrying the Orcish blade, while also insisting that she hates Orcs so much. Her reasoning is that these are good quality items she's used to, but I wonder if there's something else behind it. Some part of her that refuses to let go entirely of her upbringing, even though she was a slave and a gladiator, which she hated. Perhaps a refusal to acknowledge the universal opinion in these parts that the west is superior to the east? I can't say for sure.

'I have two murders to investigate. I should be examining the crime scenes but Lisutaris decided to advance so I can't. Do you know why Lisutaris picked this moment to move?'

Makri thinks it might have something to do with the arrival of Arichdamis from Samsarina.

'Arichdamis? King Gardos's mathematician? What does he have to do with anything?'

'I'm not sure,' says Makri. 'But he spent a long time talking in private to Lisutaris. Soon after that we were ready to move.'

'Is this something to do with his new sighting device?'

Arichdamis, as well as being a mathematician - finest in the west, according to Makri - is also a scientist and inventor. In Samsarina he was working on a new type of sight for fitting on a large, mounted crossbow, the intention being to aim the weapon rapidly and accurately enough to bring down a dragon. It was an interesting idea but I didn't think it was near to completion. Makri doesn't know anything about Arichdamis's current activities, or why he's here. I notice she keeps glancing back towards our Commanders encampment.

'Are you eager to leave?'

'No.'

'You seem nervous.'

'What do you mean, nervous?' Makri raises her voice. 'I'm not nervous. Why would I be nervous?'

'The two men who were killed. One Niojan captain, one Samsarinan major. You may remember the Samsarinan. His name was Magranos.'

Makri hesitates. 'I don't recall the name.'

'Makri, you're a terrible liar.'

'I am not a terrible liar. I've been learning your technique.'

'I can tell you're lying now.'

'That still doesn't mean I'm a terrible liar. You should learn some basic logic, Thraxas, it might help you.'

'About Magranos...'

'I knew this would happen!' cries Makri, becoming agitated. 'Someone gets murdered and it's blame the Orc woman! I'm disappointed in you, Thraxas. It's very offensive.'

'Please. Drop the outrage. You know very well why I'm suspicious. Back in Samsarina you threatened to kill Magranos.'

'I've threatened to kill a lot of people.'

'And you've killed a lot of them too. I wouldn't use that as a defence. Did you have anything to do with his death?'

'No.'

'Are you quite sure?'

'Of course I'm sure! How could I not be sure about that?'

I stare at Makri. She's uncomfortable, but whether that's from guilt, or simply annoyance at my suspicions, I can't tell. 'You hated it that he was responsible for Alceten's death.'

'Of course I did,' says Makri, hotly. 'She was murdered and no one did anything about it.'

Back in Samsarina there was an ugly affair involving fraud and bankruptcy. Young Alceten ended up dead as a result. As the affair involved important Barons it was hushed up. No charges were laid. Makri is irate at the memory. 'He should have been tried. Why should he get away with murdering a young woman just because he's chief steward to some baron?'

'The King wouldn't have let it go to trial. He couldn't afford to have his senior aristocracy dragged through the mud when the nation was gearing up for war.'

'Magranos deserved to die. But I didn't kill him.'

'If you did kill him, just tell me. It will make my life simpler. I'll keep your name out of it.'

Makri is looking increasingly angry. 'How may times do I have to say it? I didn't kill him. What about the other murder? Isn't it more likely they're connected?'

'They might be. Or they might not. Captain Istaros was at the card game hosted by General Maldon. When I left he was still healthy but he never made it back to his unit. He was found lying in the bushes, stabbed in the back. As for Magranos–'

I pause as a messenger hurries past. Lisutaris has a unit made up of young messengers who can often be seen scurrying in all directions.

'–He was found dead too. He'd been stabbed. Not in the back. In the chest. Through the heart. Quite a precise wound, according to Anumaris. Probably done by an experienced swordfighter. One that wouldn't have wanted to stab a person in the back.'

Makri prepares to become upset again. We're interrupted by the arrival of another messenger. 'Ensign Makri, Commander Lisutaris requires your presence. Captain Thraxas, she also wants you.'

The messenger hurries off. We walk towards the War Leader's tent.

'How's Lisutaris's thazis intake these days?'

'That's secret information I'm not allowed to divulge,' replies Makri, who's still annoyed at me. The guards surrounding the command tent wave us through. Inside we find Lisutaris's full command council: General Hemistos, Bishop-General Ritari and Lord Kalith-ar-Yil: the Samsarinan, Niojan and Elvish leaders of the western forces. Also in attendance are General Morgias, the Simnian commander, and Admiral Arith, commander of the joint naval forces currently tracking our progress along the southern coast. Coranius the Grinder, a powerful Turanian sorcerer, is standing beside Lisutaris. Behind him are several other senior sorcerers whose names I don't know. I recognise one of them from somewhere, a tall man, Simnian from his insignia, though I can't place him. It's an important gathering, one to which I'd not normally be invited. Nor would Arichdamis, mathematician and inventor, but he's here as well, seated by the table.

Makri takes her place close to Lisutaris. Bishop-General Ritari glowers at her. Niojans are never going to accept her because of her Orcish blood, though the other commanders seem to have become used to her. The elderly Arichdamis looks positively delighted to see her again, remembering her as a fellow mathematician. When we shared his house in Samsarina they spent most of their time talking about his calculations for pi and his new methods for measuring the areas of parabolas. Or something like that, I wasn't paying close attention. He regards me without enthusiasm, possibly remembering me as a man who demolished his food supplies. Before I have time to wonder what I'm doing here, Lisutaris brings me into the conversation. 'I've asked my Head of Security, Captain Thraxas, here for his opinion because the Captain and I fought the Orcs together seventeen years ago on the walls of Turai.'

That's quite a big build up. Better than I was expecting.

'Captain, you have intimate knowledge of Turai, and long experience of Orcish combat. I want your opinion on our current plan.'

I'm gratified. It's high time our senior officers started listening to the opinions of an experienced warrior like myself. I've always said Lisutaris was an excellent choice for War Leader. She gestures towards a map on the table that shows the walls of Turai in some detail. Radiating out from the west wall, a long line zigzags over the plains. I study the map for a few moments.

'Is that a trench? Are you planning to undermine the walls?'

'Yes. Arichdamis has provided a practical scheme, precisely calculated, whereby we approach the city via a trench, undermine the walls, and bring down a section large enough for us to enter.'

I can feel my brow creasing in a frown though I don't want to appear dismissive because I'm pleased that Lisutaris has asked for my opinion. Furthermore, I'm guessing the reason she gave me such a good introduction was because she's counting on me to support her against the doubts of her military council. Even so, the plan seems outlandish. Quite hopeless. No one has undermined a city's walls for fifty years or more. With the sorcerous power available these days, it can't be done. Every sapper, miner and worker involved would be wiped out before they got near their target.

'You're probably wondering about sorcery.' Lisutaris correctly interprets my silence. 'That's understandable. Undermining a city's walls used to be a common siege tactic but fell into disuse when sorcerers became powerful enough to destroy attackers at a distance. In this instance–' Lisutaris indicates one of the sorcerers beside Coranius. '–Dearineth the Precise Measurer has calculated that while the sorcerous powers of the Orcs and ourselves are almost exactly matched, we do hold a slight advantage. A matter of two points difference on her scale of three hundred. Not enough for us to power our way into the city. Not enough for the Orcs to repel us either. We're facing a stalemate. Or almost a stalemate. I'm proposing our slight sorcerous advantage can protect our engineers as they dig towards the walls.'

I take another look at the map. Arichdamis' projected trench approaches the city at sharp angles, zigzagging its way towards the city. It's a deep trench. In theory, the workers inside are safe from projectiles thrown by defenders. Those diggers at the furthest end of the trench, closest to the target, would be protected by a roof, strong enough to deflect rocks and arrows but light enough to be moved forward as the trench extends. Before I can give an opinion, the Elvish Lord Kalith Ar Yil speaks. 'I still don't like it, Commander. Dearineth's calculations give us only a very small advantage in sorcery. If her estimates are wrong by the merest degree, our miners will be killed. I don't want to sacrifice our engineers for no reason.'

'Dearineth the Precise Measurer is a very exact practitioner,' responds Lisutaris. 'And we have very good information from Explorer Megleth, herself an Elf.'

That doesn't fill me with confidence. Megleth works for Captain Hanama, Head of Lisutaris's Intelligence Unit. I regard them as useless. Trying not to sound negative, I ask our War Leader to clarify what she means by our sorcery cancelling out that of the Orcs. 'What will it be like for the workers in the trench? Is there going to be a whirling storm of sorcery going on around them?'

'Not a storm,' says Lisutaris. 'There may be occasional sorcerous intrusions, but we can keep them safe, using the calculations provided by Arichdamis.'

'There we disagree, Commander.' General Morgias, the Simnian commander, breaks into the conversation. 'The trench approaches the walls at a series of angles. Our senior sorcerer Gorsoman gravely doubts our ability to send sorcerous protection along such a twisted path.'

'Arichdamis has provided us with very precise calculations'

The tall Simnian sorcerer steps forward. Now I remember who he is. He's the sorcerer who was in league with Charius the Wise, back at the Sorcerers Assemblage, when Lisutaris was elected head of the guild. They were trying to have Lasat elected leader. We defeated them. I don't suppose he thinks too highly of Lisutaris as a result.

'Arichdamis is depending on his own mathematical formulae,' he says. 'Formulae which other mathematicians have not yet authenticated.'

This Simnian sorcerer Gorsoman is also a mathematician. His words increase the air of unease among the senior officers. While preparing for battle, generals don't want to be arguing about mathematical formulas no one understands.

'We've been through this already.' Lisutaris sounds impatient. 'I admit these are difficult matters but Arichdamis is unsurpassed in his field. With his calculations we can send our sorcery along the trench and protect those inside.' She turns to me again. 'Well, Captain Thraxas? Assuming we can protect the workers, what do you think?'

'If you can keep them safe, I'd say it's a promising idea. Turai's walls are difficult to storm, difficult to scale. We know that from experience. We defended them for a long time against superior forces. If our sorcerers can't overwhelm the Orcs, I don't see us getting over the walls. As for a long siege, I can see problems with that too. They're probably well supplied and they could bring in more with their dragons. So undermining the walls sounds like a good plan to me.'

I'm not at all certain it's a good plan but I'm willing to support Lisutaris against her doubters. I consult the map again. 'Personally, I'd move the trench down a little. Arichdamis has it entering just north of the palace. We'd end up bogged down if we went in there. If we breech a section a little further south we'll be in the wide park south of the palace and from there our troops can easily reach any part of the city.'

Arichdamis nods his head. 'I can make that alteration.'

The Simnian commander and his mathematical sorcerer aren't convinced but the others seem prepared to go along with Lisutaris. Admiral Arith reports on the progress of our navy. They've been shadowing us as we've moved east. As we approach Turai, a coastal city, they're not too far south of our position. Their presence is soon going to be essential for keeping the army supplied. So far they haven't faced any problems but the extent of Orcish seapower is unknown. Admiral Arith has a strong fleet, mainly Elvish. If things go well, he'll be able to prevent any Orcish ships from reinforcing the city which will be important as we lay siege. It seems to be current opinion that the Orcs won't meet us on the field before we reach Turai, preferring instead to defend the city. As the meeting breaks up, Lisutaris asks me to remain behind.

'I have news. Astrath Triple Moon. Do you know him?'

'Very well,' I reply. 'He was a friend of mine. Did he survive?'

'Yes, barely. He was trapped near the palace by Orcish sorcerers and badly injured but he made it out through the magic space just before they closed it down. He's been hiding on the coast, recovering. He managed to send word to us yesterday. Cicerius is with him.'

'Cicerius?' I'm startled. Cicerius was Deputy Consul of Turai. A decent man, as Turanian politicians go, which isn't saying that much.

'I didn't think he'd have escaped.'

'Nor did I,' admits Lisutaris. 'He's no longer young and he was never a fighter. But Astrath picked him up, half-dead apparently, and got him out. He's also been recovering, in hiding. Consul Kalius has been confirmed dead, leaving Cicerius the senior remaining Turanian politician.'

'Any word of the Royal Family?'

'None. However Astrath was close to the Palace when the Orcs entered the city and he's sure they're all dead.'

'So we have no government, apart from Cicerius.'

'It would seem so. There are a few other senators around, not many so far. We don't know if any remain captive in the city. Did you know Lodius was here?'

'Lodius? Really?' Senator Lodius was a well known politician in Turai, head of the Populares party. He's an opponent of Cicerius and dislikes the Royal Family.

'He fought his way out of the city and made it to Simnia with his own squadron. They joined up with the army on the march.'

'What's going to happen when we take Turai?' asks Makri. 'Who'll be in charge?'

That's a good question. 'If the King's dead, and his heirs, it's unclear. I don't know who's next in line.'

'Do you really think there will be another King?' wonders Lisutaris.

'Maybe. Cicerius will be senior man in the city but he's no democrat. He'd rather have another king.'

'They should put you in charge,' says Makri to Lisutaris. 'You'd be a good leader.'

The sorcerer shudders. 'When this is over all I want to do is sit in my gardens smoking my water pipe, gossiping about fashion with Tirini.'

I can sympathise with that. When this is over my only ambition is to sit in the Avenging Axe, drinking beer.

'Have you made any progress on the little matter I asked you about?' asks Lisutaris.

'Little matter? You mean the two murders?'

'Yes. The Niojans have been grumbling about it. They don't like their King's nephew dying.'

'Anumaris did some preliminary investigations but now the army's advanced it's difficult to make proper enquiries.'

'Just clear it up,' says Lisutaris, paying no regard to my difficulties. 'And make my life easier.'

Chapter Four

Back at the wagon I find a Niojan Major waiting to talk to me. He's a man of around thirty-five; fair-haired, which is unusual for a Niojan, and affable, also unusual for a Niojan. He introduces himself politely as Major Stranachus from the Niojan Intelligence Unit. He's been sent by his superiors to ask if I've made any progress with my enquiries into the death of Captain Istaros.

'Not much. The advance complicated matters.'

Major Stranachus understands. 'Of course. Difficult when you can't examine the crime scene.'

'I'm going to have to sort it out as best as I can by talking to the people involved.'

The Major asks if I'd keep him informed of any progress. I assure him I will. I've no intention of sharing any more information than I have to, but we're still being polite to each other.

'We realise you're in charge of the investigation, as the Commander's Head of Security. However my superiors will be concerned if there's no progress.' He looks at me apologetically. 'You understand why, of course.'

'Captain Istaros was the King's nephew.'

'Yes. Legate Denpir is keen to have the matter cleared up.'

Legate Denpir is the new Niojan second-in-command, replacement for Legate Apiroi who was killed in battle with the Orcs. I haven't met him yet. I'm hoping he's not as bad as Apiroi.

Major Stranachus turns to leave, then pauses. 'It was unfortunate what happened to Legate Apiroi.'

'It was. But people die in battle.'

'Of course. Though few people on our side died in *that* battle. I wouldn't have expected the Legate to be one of them.'

My internal alarm goes off, which it probably should have done already. The Niojan Legate's death is not something I'd like to become a topic of conversation.

'From what I gather, he wasn't in the front line,' continues the Major.

'I didn't really learn the circumstances...'

'Just following on behind, apparently. That was appropriate, given his rank. Yet he was killed. Curious, perhaps. Many soldiers in front of him survived. We routed the Orcs with very few casualties.'

'These things happen.' I take care to make my voice natural. 'There are always arrows flying around.'

'He died from a wound to the throat. From a blade, it's said. His body's been cremated by now, so there's no way of checking.'

'Was there any reason to check?'

The Major smiles. 'None that I know of. I just thought it was a curious death, that's all. But you're right, people always die in battle and there's no way of predicting who it will be.'

With that he departs, leaving me thoughtful. Was he making a point about Legate Apiroi or just making conversation? It was hard to tell, with his friendly manner. Damn it. I examined Apiroi's body after he died and I'm sure he didn't die at the hands of the Orcs. I found a small mark in his back which suggested he'd been killed by an assassin's dart, with the throat wound added afterwards to fool people. I've no proof, but I strongly suspect Captain Hanama murdered him on the orders of our War Leader. Legate Apiroi had been making a dangerous nuisance of himself and I've an idea that Lisutaris took the earliest opportunity of getting rid of him. I knew it might lead to trouble. Niojans aren't fools. If they learn anything incriminating it could end badly. The army could split apart if King Lamachus finds out that Lisutaris had a Niojan Legate murdered. I curse, and retreat into the wagon for a bottle of beer.

The temperature has been rising as Spring progresses. I gaze up at the sky. It's clear, only a few small clouds in the sky. Not necessarily a good thing. Last time the sky was clear there were reports of dragon activity. Flying high up, out of range, just watching us advance. I didn't see anything myself but Makri did, and a few more of the sharp-eyed Elves. I've asked Anumaris Thunderbolt to organise a visit to Captain Istaros' squadron. She's been in contact and they're expecting me. Before leaving I give my unit orders.

'We need to identify the badge Anumaris found. Rinderan, you know sorcerers from every nation. Maybe someone in your guild will be able to tell you where it came from. Anumaris, see if you can find any connection between Captain Istaros and Major Magranos. Did they know each other before this campaign started? Droo, find out how much beer each quartermaster has. I've heard rumours Turanian rations are about to be cut and I need to be prepared for emergencies. I'm off to visit the Niojans.' I scowl. I'm not keen on visiting Niojans. 'If they have a prayer call I'm ignoring it.'

'They'll be insulted.'

'Niojans are always insulted about something. We're in Abelasian territory, there's no law saying I have to obey a Niojan prayer call. Dammit, it's bad enough being in the same army. What are the Niojan sorcerers like?'

'They keep to themselves,' says Anumaris. 'They don't mix like other sorcerers.'

National boundaries don't mean as much to the Sorcerers Guild as they do to most other people. Members from all states tend to mingle freely. It doesn't surprise me the Niojans are an exception. Their sorcerers are probably worried about doing anything that might seem disloyal. The powerful Niojan church doesn't like sorcery. They'd ban it if they could. Unfortunately for them, doing that would put them at too much of a disadvantage with their neighbours.

I leave my unit to their tasks and head north through the encampment, finally passing through the Niojan cavalry division with their fine steeds and black-armoured horsemen. The troops are gathered round fires, cooking, or sitting beside their tents, attending to their weapons and armour. It's quieter than I'd have expected. Turanians or Samsarinans would be talking loudly, probably shouting friendly insults at each other over the campfires. The Niojans are more restrained. I head towards a banner with the numbers 1-6 emblazoned on it. *First Niojan Cavalry Regiment, sixth squadron.* The officer in charge, Lieutenant Namchus, greets me politely enough. He leads me to a supply tent.

'We can talk here in private,' he says.

'That's fine. Though I'll need to talk to the rest of the men as well.'

The Lieutenant looks apologetic. 'I'm sorry, that wont be possible. My orders are that only I can talk to you.'

'My orders are to investigate Captain Istaros' death. I'll need to talk to the squadron.'

'That won't be possible.' Lieutenant Namchus is polite but unwavering. I don't like it, but don't protest. I'll protest if it becomes necessary.

'When was the last time you saw Istaros?'

'Shortly after we'd eaten. Captain Istaros and I discussed the day's events together, informally, as we always did, before evening prayer call.'

'What happened after that?'

'The Captain left our encampment to visit friends.'

'You mean to attend the card game.'

The Niojan lieutenant looks pained. 'So people have said. I don't believe he was participating in any such thing.'

'Why not?'

"Captain Istaros was not a gambler.'

'I saw him there myself,' I tell him.

'There could have been other reasons he was there.'

'Are you telling me Niojan Captains aren't allowed to join in Simnian card games?'

'It's not prohibited. It is discouraged. I don't believe Captain Istaros engaged in gambling.'

Probably he concealed his liking for gambling from his unit. Maybe from his superiors too. He wouldn't be the only Niojan soldier to have done that.

'Did he have any enemies?'

'No. Captain Istaros was an fine soldier, respected by all.'

I'm dissatisfied by the lieutenant's answers. It sounds like he's simply giving me a prepared response telling me how respectable the Captain was. 'What about Major Magranos, the Samsarinan who was killed the same night? Did he know Captain Istaros?'

'I never heard Captain Istaros mention him.'

'Can you think of any reason that Magranos might have been in your encampment?'

'No.'

'Isn't it strange that two murders were carried out in your camp and none of your guards saw or heard anything?'

My questioning, having not proceeded very far, is abruptly cut short by the dragon alarm. This signal, a repetitive burst of trumpet notes, is familiar to everyone in the army. It's been drilled into us. At the signal, you take cover while the sorcerers provide a shield over the camp. I leave the tent without too much concern, presuming it's another drill, then look up to find a very large dragon hurtling out of the sky. I watch as it opens its great jaws and roars, drowning out the sound of the trumpets. I start to run, along with the Niojans around me. I risk glancing back over my shoulder. The dragon comes to an abrupt halt, striking something invisible and actually bouncing back a few metres in the sky. The air above begins to glow as the defence provided by our sorcerers gathers strength. Sorcerers have been stationed around the perimeter for just such an emergency and they've practiced their response many times. The sky turns purple as a great protective dome covers the entire encampment, repelling the dragons. It's quite a sight. Impressive but unnerving, standing underneath, unable to take action, while the hostile dragons rend and batter at the barrier, roaring with frustration as they find themselves unable to penetrate. On the plus side, and it's a big plus, our barrier is keeping out the dragons. On the negative side, we can't attack them while it's in pace. Some arrows are launched by ill-disciplined troops who've forgotten their orders but it's a futile effort. The arrows clatter against the magic barrier and fall back to earth. Neither can our own spells penetrate the shield. It stands above us, an impenetrable arc.

I'm gripping my sword tightly. Around me the Niojan troops have formed into squadrons and stand with their spears and pikes raised, the older ones looking grim, the younger one nervous. Finally the test of our endurance comes to an end. The dragons rear upwards and head east, back towards Turai. A wave of relief runs through the camp. The barrier remains in place for some time after they've gone. How long Lisutaris's sorcerers can maintain it is a military secret. As I make my way back to my wagon I'm thoughtful, and troubled. Our sorcerers held off these dragons but we're still some way from Turai. We're not yet in range of the full might of Orcish sorcerous power. When we reach Turai we're planning on laying siege to the city while digging our way in. Our sorcerers are going to have to protect us from aerial assault while also projecting some sort of additional protective field over the trench, all the way to the city walls. I hope Arichdamis has his calculations right. Otherwise, I can foresee a lot of dead miners.

Chapter Five

I eat my evening meal with the Turanian section of the Sorcerers Auxiliary Regiment, in the company of Gurd and Tanrose. Tanrose's cooking at the Avenging Axe was one of the few things that made life in Turai bearable. Her expertise also extends to producing excellent food on the move, so I eat with them as often as I can. Tanrose doesn't have access to the right sort of oven to make her famous pies, but she's still able to produce the finest stew, roast yams and assorted vegetables. She even manages to produce a decent version of her lemon cake, in a pan over the fire. It heartens me that Gurd had the good sense to ask her to marry him. The aging barbarian needed my encouragement, being too unused to the ways of romance to get it done on his own. I was pleased to help. Otherwise Tanrose and her cooking skills might have been poached by a competitor, something I couldn't allow. Recently Gurd told me they were planning on producing a baby. I'm happy for them, providing I don't have to talk about it. Fortunately, today's dragon attack is the only topic of conversation around the campfire. Those who've never been to war were unnerved by the sight of the huge beasts. Those who've experienced them before take heart from the way our sorcerers repelled them.

'Lisutaris has them well organised,' I say. 'Best defensive shield I've ever seen, put up at short notice.'

Gurd agrees, but points out that it wasn't a full-scale attack. 'Only twelve dragons or so, more like an expedition to check our defences.'

'True, but Amrag will know he can't chase us off easily now.'

Gurd still has doubts. 'We're going to end up outside the city walls with every dragon in the east hovering overhead. One mistake by the sorcerers and we're done for. What happens when we get into the city? Lisutaris won't be able to keep the shield in place when we're fighting in the streets.'

'I suppose she has some plan. We have to get into the city first. That's going to be difficult enough, with the trench, and

Arichdamis doing mathematics to help the sorcery, or whatever it was.'

'I hear Makri's helping Arichdamis,' says Tanrose.

I raise my eyebrows. 'Really? I wonder why she didn't tell me that?'

'Probably because you always make fun of Arichdamis and his mathematics. And Makri and her mathematics.'

'I may have made the odd flippant comment.' I'm feeling genial as I load up with another bowl of stew, deftly grabbing the last roasted yam before anyone else can lay their hands on it. My mood dissipates as Captain Hanama appears. Our War Leader's Head of Intelligence is about as welcome as an Orc at an Elvish wedding while I'm eating my dinner.

'Captain Thraxas.' Hanama is softly spoken. I've never liked it. 'I need a word with you in private.'

I'm scowling as I haul myself to my feet. Anything that brings Hanama here can only be bad news. We withdraw behind a row of tents where the flickering firelight casts our shadows on the canvas. My shadow is huge in comparison to Hanama's.

'You better have some good reason for disturbing my dinner.'

Hanama regards me coldly. 'My intelligence unit has learned something troubling concerning the murder of Major Magranos. Baron Vosanos has let it be known in private he suspects Makri was involved.' Hanama is studying me as I take this in. 'You don't seem surprised.'

'It's not unexpected. Makri did express a desire for revenge.'

'Revenge? For what?'

I give Hanama the details. 'Magranos was most likely responsible for the death of the young woman Alceten, back in Samsarina. Makri didn't like it that he wouldn't be brought to justice.'

'Did he actually kill Alceten?'

'He probably arranged her murder. There was no proof. Even if there had been, he wouldn't have been prosecuted. Magranos was acting on behalf of Baron Vosanos and Barons don't get prosecuted for murder in Samsarina.'

'We can't allow Makri to be implicated in a murder. Have you any better suspects?'

'What do you mean *better*? More likely to have done it? Or just more convenient to blame?'

'Either,' says Captain Hanama.

I have no better suspects. I don't have any suspects at all. Hanama isn't satisfied. 'Shouldn't you have found out something by now?'

'Stick to intelligence, Captain Hanama. Leave investigating to me.'

'Why? Is there any proof you have a talent for it?'

I stare icily at her. 'I'm number one chariot at investigating.'

'So you've been known to say. I've never heard anyone else agree. Makri cannot be arrested, Captain Thraxas. Not while she's so closely associated with our Commander.'

Hanama seems over-insistent about all this. She has been before, about Makri. I thank her tersely for her information then head back to the campfire. Tanrose has saved me a piece of lemon cake. I appreciate it though I'm troubled as I eat. I don't like it that Makri's name is being whispered in connection with Magranos' death because I'm not certain she didn't kill him. She might have, given the chance. Despite the excellence of Tanrose's cooking, the evening ends on a gloomy note. Gurd's platoon is running short of beer and can spare me only one bottle. It's inadequate for a man of my appetites.

'Sorry, Thraxas,' says Gurd. 'We're being rationed. Quartermaster says we might run out soon.'

I look at my empty flagon. 'How are we meant to function without beer? Am I meant to storm the walls of Turai sober? Ridiculous notion. Who ever did that?'

Gurd laughs. 'Not you, that's for sure.'

On the way back to my wagon I'm pensive. It's worrying news that there might be a beer shortage. It's all very well for the Turanian quartermaster to tell us that shortages are inevitable in wartime, but I'm not convinced they tried hard enough. Anumaris is waiting for me beside the wagon. 'I don't think they put in enough effort,' I tell her.

'Pardon?'

'The Turanian quartermasters. Yes, it's wartime. And yes, they had to stock up in a foreign land after the city fell. But is that really an excuse for running out of beer before the campaign's over? Did they try to avert this catastrophe? Did they examine all possible avenues? Probably not, with Lisutaris as Commander. Wouldn't surprise me if she instructed them not to bring enough. I'm sure their wagons could have carried more beer.'

'Perhaps they required storage space for weapons and armour.'

'A flimsy excuse. I tell you Anumaris, it wouldn't have happened in my day. The city's been going downhill for years. No wonder the Orcs beat us. Well, I'm defeated. I can't go on. I'm going to lie in my tent and think of the old days when generals had enough sense to bring enough beer for the army.'

'But I have information,' protests Anumaris, as I attempt to leave.

'Is it about beer?'

'No! It's about the investigation!' Anumaris raises her voice 'Information you asked for. Information I strived to find out quickly.'

'Right. I was forgetting. Well, let's hear it.'

Anumaris produces a rectangle of parchment, covered in her neat writing. 'Captain Istaros, nephew of the King of Nioj, visited Elath in Samsarina for the swordfighting tournament. While there, he made enquiries about buying a plot of land to build a house. He was referred to Baron Vosanos, who had land to sell, and thereby met the Baron's chief steward, Magranos, with whom he concluded the deal. The land was bought and paid for. As far as anyone is aware, there were no difficulties in what was a simple transaction. Some weeks later, Istaros and Magranos, now both members of their respective nation's armies, became re-acquainted with each other. It's not known how they met again, whether deliberately or by chance. However, it wasn't a secret. They were observed together. So they did know each other, and their deaths could be connected, though they occurred some hours apart.' Anumaris turns over the page. She has a lot of notes. 'No one I talked to had noticed anything suspicious about either Istaros or Magranos, but I did learn there might have been some sort of incident in Elath.'

'What sort of incident?'

'One of the cooks told me he'd heard Captain Istaros was in a fight in Samsarina, and came back with a freshly healed wound. No one else knew anything about that.'

That's a lot of information, gathered in a short space of time. I congratulate Anumaris on her work. As I'm doing so, Rinderan appears. Unlike Anumaris, Rinderan's appearance has changed over the course of the campaign. He's no longer the neat young sorcerer he was when he arrived in my unit. His hair is longer, and tousled. The sword at his hip is slung a fraction lower, like the experienced fighters in the Sorcerers Auxiliary Regiment. He's swapped his rather fancy sorcerer's rainbow cloak for a much more muted version which is slung back over his shoulders in a businesslike fashion. He might almost be described as dashing, though he's not quite old enough to carry that off.

'I made a discovery, Captain Thraxas.' He takes out the badge Anumaris found. 'This comes from the personal defence unit recruited by Bishop-General Ritari.'

'Are you sure?'

'A Niojan sorcerer who owes me a favour identified it for me. There aren't many of them around, according to her. The Bishop-General gave them out to his unit. I'm not sure if they even wear them in public. It's something of am unofficial unit.'

I take the badge in my hands. 'The personal defence unit of Bishop-General Ritari. What do you make of that?'

'That Captain Istaros was a member of the unit?'

'Maybe.' I turn to Anumaris. 'What do you think?'

'He might have been. What if the killer dropped it? Could Bishop-General Ritari's defence unit have been involved in the murder?'

'Impossible to say. It might have been planted there to throw suspicion on them. Droo? Any ideas?'

Droo has been sipping surreptitiously from a bottle of Elvish wine she's obtained from somewhere. She doesn't have any ideas. I sit down at the front of our wagon. At a moment like this I'd usually have some intuition as to what's been going on. A feeling for where the badge came from. Unfortunately my intuition is telling me nothing.

'So we have a badge found at the scene of Captain Istaros's murder. Anumaris, find out if it belonged to Istaros, or someone else. What about the murder of Major Magranos? Any information regarding that?'

Everyone looks blank. I expect I'm looking blank too. It's not as if this is the most baffling case I've ever encountered but for some reason I can't seem to get started. Anumaris looks up from her notes. 'Captain Thraxas, was there any indication at the card game that Captain Istaros was in danger? Was he distracted?'

'I can't remember.' My security unit is not impressed by my memory failure, though they don't come right out and say it.

'Did anything happen there that might shed some light on the murders?'

'Not that I recall. Nothing unusual happened.'

'You got into a fight,' says Droo.

'As I said, nothing unusual.' I shake my head. I need to be able to nose around a crime scene to get an idea of what's been happening. Trying to solve crime at a distance is a new experience. I don't like it.

'Are we sure Major Magranos didn't visit the card game?' asks Rinderan. Everyone looks at me.

'I'm fairly sure he wasn't there. I wouldn't bet the kingdom on it.'

'I hear Makri's a suspect,' says Droo, alarmingly.

'What? Where did you hear that?'

'From an Elf in the intelligence unit.'

'Damn that intelligence unit! Hanama's people are probably blabbing to everyone.'

Anumaris asks why Makri would be a suspect. I tell her about Makri's threats, back in Samsarina, and Baron Vosanos's suspicions.

'Did Makri threaten him in public?'

'I thought she'd only mentioned it to me and Lisutaris. I don't know how word got out. Maybe she did mention it to someone else. It's bad. We cant have our War Leader's bodyguard suspected

36

of murdering a Samsarinan officer, no matter how much he deserved it.' I take a sip from Droo's wine. It's Elvish, not one of their finest bottles but not bad at that.

'I have more bad news,' says Anumaris. 'The Niojan intelligence officer, Major Stranachus. He's suspicious about the death of Legate Apiroi. He's been asking questions.'

My eyes narrow a fraction. 'Why exactly would that be bad news?'

'Because...' Anumaris doesn't complete the sentence.

'Because we all think Commander Lisutaris and Captain Hanama were behind it,' says Droo, brightly.

'Never say that again!'

'It's true.'

'It might be true but don't say it. We can't have the Niojans going off in a huff because our Commander got rid of their King's senior representative.'

'Do you think she did?' asks Anumaris.

'Possibly. I don't think it could be proved.'

'I heard though my guild that Major Stranachus has been talking to some of the Niojan sorcerers. He might be hoping they could look back in time and see how the Legate died.'

I shake my head. Everything just became worse. Life was simpler when I was in the middle of a phalanx, holding a spear. I never volunteered to sort out complicated matters of state. It's not something I'm good at. 'I need to talk to Lisutaris. Before that I'll need a decent bottle of beer.'

Anumaris shakes her head. 'You can't drink beer before talking to Lisutaris.'

'Who says I can't?'

'Lisutaris. And me.'

'To hell with you both. Droo, round up every beer in the area.'

Anumaris rises, places her hand on Droo's shoulder, physically preventing her from rising. 'Our Commander forbade you drinking to excess and instructed me to make sure you didn't.'

Anumaris seems to be learning to stand up for herself. I don't like it. I shake my head again, swiftly locate a bottle of beer I hid near the campfire, and storm off, annoyed at everything. No one tells Thraxas he can't drink beer. I'll have something to say to Lisutaris about this. At this moment, trumpets sound the advance.

'Dammit.' I'm obliged to turn round and march back to the wagon. Droo is already attaching the horses. Rinderan is magically throwing our belongings in the back. Anumaris glares at me. 'Do you have beer hidden everywhere?'

'No. I've drunk most of it. I have a few left for emergencies.'

I climb into the wagon. Droo jerks the reins, and we trundle forward with the rest of the army, now only a few miles from the border of the City State of Turai.

Chapter Six

Dragons continue to track our progress; young, fast beasts, high above, out of range of sorcery. The army is wary though we're becoming used to them. Neither the light, skirmishing troops posted along our flanks nor our advance scouts report any other enemy activity. We advance through the afternoon, travelling over territory familiar to every Turanian exile. We've crossed the River Turisa which marks the eastern border of the city-state. Turai itself is less than fifty miles from here. After a brief climb through low hills we come into farmland, normally fertile, but now bare. It should be coming to life with wheat and barley but the farmers have fled and the crops remain unplanted. If we come through this, the population of Turai will have problems feeding itself in the coming year. I banish the thought; we have more to worry about at the moment.

Our advance halts in the late evening. I leave the wagon and hurry towards Lisutaris's position. Her command tent is already in place, erected by sorcery. If I can get there quickly enough I might be able to talk to her before she's involved in her endless meetings with her senior officers. My progress is interrupted by Makri, who's carrying papers and looking unhappy.

'I'm feeling stupid,' she says.

From a woman who's never shown any qualms about displaying her intelligence, it's an unusual statement. 'Why?'

Makri waves the papers in my face. 'Arichdamis's mathematics. It's so complicated.'

'Didn't you know that already?'

'This is even more complicated than I imagined. He's creating a pathway for sorcery to protect the trench. It involves working out the volumes of all these interconnecting cones and it takes so many calculations.' Makri screws up her face. 'He's invented this new sort of mathematics. I'm trying to master it but it's hard to get peace to study.'

I'm sympathetic to a degree, though not actually displeased to learn that Makri isn't the smartest mathematician in the entire world. Sometimes I worry she might be. 'Do you need to learn it all? Won't Arichdamis do his own calculations?'

'I'm meant to check everything for errors. I'm second back-up as well.'

'Second back-up?'

'Arichdamis recruited a sorcerer from Samsarina, Lezunda Blue Glow. He's meant to take over if anything happens to him. I'm next in line.'

'Then lets hope Lisutaris is protecting them both with her finest spells.'

'What does that mean?'

I'm about to tell Makri that if I have to run into a trench in hostile territory protected only by her mathematics, I don't give myself much chance of coming out of it alive, but I bite my tongue. I don't seem to get as much pleasure out of insulting her intellectual aspirations as I used to. I don't know why. 'You'll be fine,' I say instead. 'And Arichdamis is tough for an elderly mathematician. I'm sure he'll see us through. Is his plan any good?'

Makri screws up her face. 'I think so. We can't just lay a big sorcerous protection field right over the trench because it won't be strong enough, not at the front line where it actually touches the city walls. All the Orcish sorcerers will be trying to destroy it. Arichdamis says he can calculate a channel to funnel in concentrated sorcerous protection, even though the trench is zigzagging so he has to send the sorcery round corners. If his figures are right, it should work.'

'What if they're wrong?'

'Everyone in the trench will be killed. Torn to shreds, probably. I don't think they're planning to tell the diggers that.'

'Probably best not to.'

We walk towards Lisutaris's command tent. 'We wouldn't have imagined this happening the first time you appeared in the Avenging Axe,' I say.

'I was only looking for a safe place to stay for a few nights before finding somewhere better. I never saw myself as a tavern wench.'

'Now here we are, practically leading the armies. Although I'm not surprised I've ended up in an important position. I'm one of the few decent men left in the west.'

'Arichdamis still shudders at the damage you did to his cellars.'

'That was really more Baron Girimos than me. His appetite was insatiable. I wasn't the only one who annoyed Arichdamis. I remember a particular look of disgust on his face when you vomited over his couch.'

Makri looks guilty. 'He *was* disturbed about that but it's all right now since I blamed it on you. I told him you led me astray.'

'Did he believe that?'

'Very readily,' says Makri. 'Lisutaris backed me up with tales of your past deprivations.'

'I'm sure she exaggerated.'

'There was really no need.'

The delay caused by my conversation with Makri means I've missed the opportunity to talk to Lisutaris. Senior officers are already gathering outside her tent, waiting to consult her. Bishop-General Ritari and General Hemistos walk past me with barely an acknowledgement. To their surprise and mine, they're halted by Lisutaris who appears at the entrance, spots me, and waves me through. 'Captain Thraxas. Urgent matters of security. Inside immediately.'

General Hemistos and Bishop-General Ritari find themselves hanging round the entrance while I saunter past, pleased to have the public reminded that Captain Thraxas is not a man to be ignored. Makri follows me. Inside, Lisutaris is fumbling around with her purse.

'You're probably wondering what security matter calls for this, eh… important meeting.'

'It's an excuse to keep Ritari and Hemistos out of your tent because you're desperate for thazis.'

'Very astute, Thraxas.' Lisutaris drags a small bag of thazis from her purse, separates a few strands and rolls them into a stick with one hand in a movement so quick it's hard to follow. She snaps her fingers, lighting it by sorcery, and then inhales deeply.

'I couldn't get a moment's peace during the advance,' she tells us, exhaling smoke. 'Damned Elvish messengers every few minutes, and if it wasn't them it was Admiral Arith with some urgent naval news. I simply could not face the Bishop-General without some support.'

Finishing her thazis stick, the sorceress immediately rolls another. I notice some alarm on Makri's face. Lisutaris's thazis intake was meant to be diminishing. On this display, it might not be.

'Maybe you should just tell the Bishop-General you're in charge and you're going to smoke thazis whether he likes it or not.'

'He'd spread it around that I'm dependent on it. It wouldn't look good. You know what puritans these Niojans are. Not that Samsarinans are any better when it comes to thazis. Damn them all.'

Lisutaris rolls and lights another stick. I've no objection to acting as a distraction to enable our War Leader to soak up her favourite drug, but I did come here on business. 'There are some things you should know, concerning my investigation.'

'I doubt that,' replies the sorceress. 'I told you to make it go away and not bother me.'

'Circumstances make that difficult.'

'Then change the circumstances.' Lisutaris finishes her third stick of thazis. The air is thick with the pungent smell. She mutters a word and the aroma disappears. She's got all aspects of her habit well covered. 'Now, I have to talk to Hemistos and Ritari, so if you'll excuse me–'

I'm not prepared to be brushed off so easily. 'Afraid not, Commander. There are some things you have to hear whether you like it or not.'

Our War Leader glares at me. 'Whatever it is I don't have time.'

'Baron Vosanos suspects that Makri killed Major Magranos. Magranos was the Baron's chief steward so he's unlikely to let it drop. He's been talking about it in public so the rumour's probably spreading through Samsarinan ranks. General Hemistos will hear it soon enough.'

Lisutaris shakes her head in annoyance. 'This is exactly the sort of thing you're meant to deal with. I'm sure Makri didn't kill this Magranos. And even if she did–'

'I didn't.'

'–I don't want to know about it. I can't be distracted with petty matters like this. Deal with it. Make it disappear.'

I don't like it that Lisutaris disregards my problems so easily. I don't like that she doesn't care about the murder either. I've always had this odd fixation that murders shouldn't go unpunished. 'I'll do my best. But that's not your only problem. It's not your worst problem either. Your worst problem is Major Stranachus.'

'Who's that?'

'A Niojan intelligence officer. Rather a clever man. He suspects there was something untoward in the death of Legate Apiroi.'

For the first time, I have Lisutaris's full attention. 'What do you mean?'

'He suspects he wasn't killed in battle.'

'Ridiculous,' scoffs Lisutaris. 'There was a battle. He was killed. What is there to be suspicious about?'

'A small mark on Apiroi's back which suggested he might have been killed by a poisoned dart rather than an enemy blade. I saw it. Whether anyone else did, I don't know. The body's gone now but there might be another witness for all I know.'

'You're not making much sense here, Captain Thraxas.' Our Commander's voice has gone cold.

'I'm making good sense. I've suspected all along that Legate Apiroi was murdered and the battle provided a convenient excuse for getting rid of him. I remember he was blackmailing you at the time.'

'Are you inferring I was behind it?'

'It's a natural inference. You were in an awkward position.'

Lisutaris draws herself up to her full height so she can look down at me. 'Captain Thraxas, it's fortunate we share a certain amount of history. Otherwise you'd be liable to find yourself on a permanent visit to the stockade for gross insubordination.'

'Legate Apiroi was King Lamachus's personal representative.'

'He was an annoying troublemaker with a dangerous amount of ambition.'

'If the Niojans find out you sent Hanama to kill him then we're in a lot of trouble.'

'Fortunately, I didn't do that. So there will be no trouble.'

I look our Commander in the eye. 'Major Stranachus has been talking to the Niojan sorcerers. It's likely he's asking them if they can look back in time to see the murder. That wouldn't be easy, with the moons being in such bad alignment, but you never know, a specialist might be able to do it. They could get lucky and find a good, clear picture of the whole chain of events. It's happened before.'

Lisutaris regards me calmly for a moment, then turns to Makri. 'Ensign Makri, ask my aide-de-camp to come in.'

Makri disappears outside for a few seconds, returning with Julius, the young Turanian captain who acts as our War Leader's assistant.

'Captain Julius. Issue this order immediately. '*To all sorcerers currently with the army, in all regiments. The use of sorcery for all non war-related purposes is henceforth prohibited. As our full power is necessary for maintaining protection and defeating the enemy, no other spells - historical, oracular, messaging, or otherwise - may be used without the express permission of Commander Lisutaris, War Leader. This order will remain in place until further notice.*'

One of Captain Julius' skills is his ability to rapidly take dictation. He finishes copying down the order almost as soon as Lisutaris stops speaking. 'I'll have this distributed immediately, Commander.' He salutes smartly and hurries from the tent.

'You're forbidding sorcery?'

'For all non war-related matters, yes. The guild will obey me, and I'll be notified of any breeches of my command.'

'Won't people be suspicious?'

'I don't see why,' says Lisutaris. 'It's common for sorcerers to preserve their power till it's required in wartime. Not that there's anything to be suspicious about anyway. And now, Captain Thraxas, I really must confer with my senior officers. Please ensure all these problems are dealt with in a manner which causes me no further distraction.'

With that, Lisutaris shows me the exit. I trudge back towards my wagon. The sky is grey. It's warm and muggy. I feel like a beer. Close to the wagon Droo appears, greeting me cheerfully. Her dull green tunic, spotless and new when she embarked with the Elvish fleet, is now creased and worn, fraying at the edges. Along with the other Elves she's come through a sea voyage, a battle and a long march. They're starting to look as tattered as the rest of the army.

'Someone's waiting for you.'

'Who?'

'Sreepa. Or something like that.'

'Sareepa?' I make a rapid about-turn. 'Time for me to patrol.'

'Thraxas, you dog! Stop right there!'

I turn around reluctantly. There stands Sareepa Lightning Strikes the Mountain, powerful sorcerer, once again not looking that pleased to see me. 'If you try sneaking off I'll drag you back here with a spell.'

'Really? I happen to be wearing a fine spell protection charm.'

'I happen to be the head of the Matteshan Sorcerers Guild and I'll wager my power against any charm cheap enough for you to own.'

There appears to be no way of avoiding Sareepa. 'Bring help,' I mutter to Droo, then trudge the final distance to the wagon. Sareepa is standing with her arms folded. She's a strong looking woman, broad shouldered, as tall as me, and her rainbow cloak has the functional appearance of a sorcerer who doesn't waste time on fripperies.

'Sareepa! You're looking well.'

She scowls at me. 'Don't try and compliment me, you dog.'

I raise my eyebrows. 'Is that any way to talk to an old companion? How old were we when we met? I must have been nineteen, you can't have been much more than sixteen.'

'And you were a treacherous piece of work even then.' She glowers at me. 'Well?'

'Well what?'

'What do you have to say for yourself about almost killing me at the Sorcerers Assemblage?'

'I don't remember that happening...'

'I ended up in an alcoholic stupor after you tricked me into drinking half a bottle of over-strength klee laced with dwa! I damned near died. I would have if the medical sorcerers in Turai hadn't got to me in time. Fortunately they weren't as useless as everyone else in your city.'

'Well, really Sareepa. There was a lot of drinking going on at the Sorcerers Assemblage. If you overindulged, I don't see how it can be blamed on me. I was simply there to extend hospitality.'

Sareepa bridles. 'You were there to cheat by every means possible so that Lisutaris was elected head of the guild. Which in my case meant rendering me so intoxicated I allowed my delegation to vote for her.'

I spread my arms wide. 'I wouldn't say *cheat* was the appropriate word. I admit I tried to use what little influence I could muster, but not in an unfair way.'

Sareepa abruptly laughs. I remain on guard, unable to tell if her mood has brightened or if she's just preparing for another assault. Sorcerers can be erratic and hard to read.

'You, Makri, that woman Tilupasis - you flooded the assemblage with so much gold, alcohol, dwa, thazis and whores I'm surprised you didn't kill us all.'

'And look how well it turned out! Lisutaris is a fine head of the guild. She's a great War Leader. It's lucky for us she was elected.'

Sensing a slight softening of relations, I usher Sareepa towards one of the small wooden chairs beside the wagon, then grope around under the wheels.

'What the hell are you doing?' demands Sareepa.

I pull out two bottles of beer.

'You have to hide your beer? Why?'

'There's a shortage. And other reasons I won't go into.' I hand one bottle to Sareepa and sit down beside her.

'How do you know I'm drinking again?' she asks.

'Because I knew you when you were sixteen. Honestly, I did you a favour at the assemblage. You'd fallen under the influence of that idiotic sorcerer from Nioj, Almalas. He was such a puritan. All these Niojans are. Don't drink, don't smoke thazis, don't do anything that might make life tolerable. It was an act of friendship releasing you from his clutches.'

Sareepa opens the bottle and drinks. 'I know. I'm embarrassed thinking about it. I don't know what got into me. That doesn't excuse you almost killing me.' Sareepa brushes a strand of hair away from her face. Most of the female sorcerers tie their long hair back neatly while on military duty, but Sareepa lets hers spill over her shoulders. Perhaps it's a sign of her status as Head of the Matteshan Sorcerers Guild. Lisutaris likewise maintains her normal coiffure. According to Makri, our War Leader spends a few minutes every day alone with her friend Tirini to attend to hair and make-up, neither of which they're prepared to ignore entirely, despite the war.

As Sareepa's mood starts to thaw, I remember why I used to like her. She was a wild youth. We did a lot of drinking together. That didn't prevent her from making progress with her sorcery. She went on to be powerful while I failed hopelessly as an apprentice.

'Where has our War Leader assigned you?' I ask.

'The trench. Seems like a strange plan to me, digging our way in, but I'm not going to argue about it. I'm part of the team sending out the protective sorcery while they dig. Lisutaris has me, Coranius, Tirini, a few others, all assigned to protecting the trench as it goes towards the walls.'

'That's a lot of sorcerous power.'

'I hope it's worth it. Apparently our magic has to be directed by some mathematical system no one knows anything about.' Sareepa frowns. 'Seems risky to me, it could blow up in our faces. Any more beer?'

'I'll check.'

'You'll check? You don't know? What's the matter with you?'

'One, there's a general beer shortage. Two, Anumaris Thunderbolt. She's fanatically anti-beer, encouraged by Lisutaris. Food rationing and no beer. I'm fading away to a shadow.' This is an exaggeration, but I have lost some weight. The escape from Turai, the long march back, the lack of a regular supply of beer and the wartime scarcity of Tanrose's pies has all had a detrimental effect. 'My clothes are hanging off me.'

Sareepa laughs. 'You're slightly smaller than I remember. I wouldn't say you were fading away.'

A swift examination of Droo's tent reveals no beer but I do find two bottles of Elvish wine tucked away. I spend the next hour drinking these with Sareepa, reminiscing about our younger days and discussing our prospects in the war. It vaguely occurs to me that I should be investigating something but I can't raise any enthusiasm. When we've finished our wine, Sareepa rises to her feet. 'Time for me to go. I have to take lessons, if you can believe it. New techniques for sending sorcery through artificial dimensions as calculated by Arichdamis. It's all starting to sound worse, the more I think about it.'

Sareepa departs unwillingly to her lessons. Having spent a pleasant afternoon drinking, idling, and gossiping, I can think of no better plan than a prolonged nap before dinner. I head for the wagon to lie down. Before I reach it Makri arrives. She's carrying a sheaf of papers and looking unhappy. 'Droo said you were about to be murdered by Sareepa.'

'You took your time coming to rescue me.'

Makri shrugs. 'I figured you'd be all right. You usually manage to talk your way out of things.'

'I could have been in serious–'

'But enough of your problems,' says Makri. 'I've got real troubles.' She looks despairingly at the sheaf of papers in her hand. 'I can't do these damned calculations.'

'I'm sure you can.'

'No, I can't. It's too complicated. Arichdamis is now inventing more new fields of mathematics.' She sighs. 'I can't keep up. No one could.'

'What about that sorcerer that's helping him? Lezunda Blue Glow?'

'Apparently he can.' Makri sounds sour. 'Another mathematical genius to demonstrate I'm not as smart as I thought I was.'

I attempt to be encouraging. 'You just need more time. You've always been top student, I'm sure you can do it. Have some thazis, it'll calm you down.'

Makri inhales deeply on the thazis stick. 'I was top student at Guild College. That's like junior arithmetic compared to this.' Makri waves a sheet of unintelligible figures at me. 'Look at this. To protect the trench as it zigzags, Arichdamis needs to pretend the sorcery goes through extra dimensions. Well not *pretend*, exactly. They're sort of there. But they're sort of not there as well.'

'Like the magic space?'

'Something like that. Except you can't enter them.'

'But the sorcery is meant to go through them?'

'Sort of. But not really. It's imaginary. But necessary for the calculations.' Makri points to one of the pages in the middle of her bundle. 'This is the start of the required calculation to send the sorcery into the second new dimension.'

The paper is covered in symbols I don't recognise. It's not like any writing I've ever seen.

'And that's only the start of the second dimension,' says Makri. 'Getting through it is worse.'

'How many of these extra dimension are there?'

'Three so far. Arichdamis keeps discovering more.' Makri finishes the thazis stick and starts rolling another. 'I can't keep up. I'm meant to be checking the figures but I can't do it.'

Looking at Makri's sheets of paper, I can appreciate her problem. 'Does it matter? If Arichdamis and Lezunda can do it? As long as they get everything right, you won't be called into action.'

Makri nods, gloomily. 'I'm hoping that happens. But it's made me realise how stupid I am. What was I thinking, imagining I could go to the university? Obviously it's a silly notion. I'll just have to be a barmaid all my life.'

'You're over-reacting. You'll get the hang of it.'

'I won't. I'm too stupid.'

Makri's self-esteem seems to have taken a severe knock. The revelation that she's a long way behind Arichdamis and Lezunda Blue Glow in mathematics has damaged her confidence.

'God help us if anything happens to them,' she says. 'Because if Lisutaris asks me to step in then we'll really be in trouble. We'll have a trench full of dead engineers, killed by the first Orcish spell that comes our way. Or the first Orcish arrow. Any hostile artefact, really. My hopeless attempts won't keep anything out. Probably won't even have to wait for an Orcish attack; the engineers will all be dead from our own sorcery because my useless calculations will make it arrive through the wrong dimension and kill them all. I might wipe out the entire army.'

'Makri, I think you're going too far here. I'm sure you're not going to wipe out the army.'

'Wait till Lisutaris's sorcery starts bursting out of another dimension because I didn't notice it was there. Things are looking bad, Thraxas. I should never have pretended I was any good at mathematics. I should have studied something else at Guild College. The child's painting class. That's more my level.'

There was a time when I enjoyed mocking Makri's academic pretensions. I don't do that as often these days. She puts in so much effort it doesn't seem amusing any more. I try to think of something more encouraging to say but such is her depression it's difficult to know what. We sit in silence for a few minutes, smoking thazis.

'What did Sareepa want?' asks Makri, after a while.

'Just reminiscing about old times. She complimented my figure.'

'What?'

'Told me I was in good shape. Not a surprise, I always did think Sareepa had a thing for me.'

'The Head of the Matteshan Sorcerers Guild has a thing for you?'

'She wasn't head of their guild when I met her. Just a young ruffian fond of drink and trouble. Back in those days, I was an expert on both. I expect she's remembered me fondly for a long time.'

Makri shakes her head, but it does raise a smile, which is some improvement. She departs in a slightly better mood, still clutching her sheaf of papers, resolving to make an another attempt at understanding Arichdamis's convoluted calculations. It's finally time for my long-overdue afternoon sleep. I've almost made it into the safety of the wagon when one of Lisutaris's young messengers arrives at a run. 'Captain Thraxas. Commander Lisutaris requires your presence immediately.'

There's no use protesting. I can't refuse a direct order. Grumbling angrily about the poor state of affairs when a man can't be left alone for five minutes to rest his eyes, I trudge the short distance back to the command centre.

Chapter Seven

Huddled around the entrance to Lisutaris's command tent are a group of fifteen people. It's an unlikely gathering. There's a young soldier from the Samsarinan cavalry, an Elf from their Reconnaissance Regiment, a woman whom I've seen unloading supplies at the Simnian military kitchen, another woman wearing the uniform of the Kamaran medical unit, a Niojan infantryman and various others. Not all of them are military people. Some are dressed in civilian clothes, part of the support staff who follow along behind the army. I'm puzzled as to why they've been summoned by Lisutaris. None of them, apart from myself, would seem to be important to the war effort. Close by are two sorcerers, Coranius the Grinder and Tirini Snake Smiter. Coranius looks more hostile than usual. Tirini looks bored, though she is resplendent in a shimmering rainbow cloak, blue high heeled boots and a collection of dragon scale jewellery. Neither acknowledge me. Moments after I arrive, Lisutaris appears. The gathering regards her anxiously, wondering why they've been summoned.

Lisutaris wastes no time getting down to business. 'I've called you because each of you has some sorcerous skill and we need to use it.'

The group edges backwards, apprehension on their faces. 'This must be a mistake, Commander,' says the Samsarinan cavalryman, quite boldly in the circumstances. 'I have no sorcerous power.'

'Yes, you do.' Lisutaris contradicts him. 'You attended the Samsarinan college for sorcerers apprentices for eight months when you were nineteen.'

'I failed every part of the course, Commander.'

'No matter. You learned the basics and you retain that knowledge.' Lisutaris turns to the Simnian kitchen worker. 'Your mother was a sorcerer and taught you several spells while you were a child.'

The kitchen worker goes pale, probably imagining she's about to be hurled into combat with the Orcish Sorcerers Guild. 'I've never practiced or studied, Commander.'

'It doesn't matter. I've made enquiries and you possess some power. As do you, Private Yanachus. You were an apprentice for five months before your parents, not approving of sorcery, made you withdraw. All of you have some degree of sorcerous experience, enough to control these.' Lisutaris nods to her aide Captain Julius. The Captain steps forward, carrying a fancy embroidered bag, and starts handing out small, flat pieces of slate, each about three inches square. I take one and examine it. It's inscribed in a language I can't read. There's a moment's silence as everyone studies their slates and wonders what they're for.

Lisutaris draws herself up, looking grand. 'As we approach Turai, the likelihood of dragon attack increases. So far, my sorcerers have successfully shielded us. As we reach our destination, certain members of the Sorcerers Guild will be required for other duties. To make up for this, you sixteen will assist with maintaining our anti-dragon shield, using the objects you've been given. Each slate acts as a sorcerous relay, boosting the shield as required. All you have to do is point them at the sky and let our sorcerers do the rest. Tirini Snake Smiter and Coranius the Grinder will give you further instructions. Are there any questions?'

There are plenty of questions. The terrifying prospect of suddenly finding themselves part of the dragon shield loosens everyone's tongues. The assembly, previously intimidated in front of our War Leader, now bombard her with anxious queries.

'Will it be dangerous?' Will it happen often? What if it doesn't work?'

'What if I'm busy doing something else? My Captain won't like me leaving my unit.'

'Do we have to do it? I'm scared of dragons!'

Our War Leader holds up her hand. 'Enough! Yes, you have to do it. Regard it as a privilege. I don't know how often it will happen. That depends on the Orcs. It will work if you all do it properly. This takes priority over anything else. Your officers will be informed of that. And yes, it may be dangerous. Everything in wartime is dangerous. If we lose we're all going to die, by dragon or by other means, so make sure you do your best to avoid defeat.'

Lisutaris turns her gaze on the Kamaran nurse. 'Of course you're scared of dragons,' she says, not particularly sympathetically. 'It would be foolish not to be. If we don't stop the Orcs now there will be dragons in Kamara soon enough. So make sure you play your part.'

I wouldn't say this was the most rousing speech I've ever heard. The unfortunate souls who've been selected don't look particularly re-assured though they fall silent, resigned to their fate.

'Tirini and Coranius will instruct you further,' says Lisutaris briskly. She turns to me. 'Captain Thraxas, I assume you need no further instruction? You should know how the sorcerous relay works.'

I glance down at the piece of slate. I'm meant to guard the army against dragon attacks by waving it in the air. I can see that ending well. I let out a sigh. 'I'm aware of how it works, Commander.'

'Good. Follow me, I have other business with you.'

I trudge after Lisutaris into her command tent, leaving behind a group of fifteen unwilling volunteers receiving instructions from two powerful sorcerers. Tirini still looks bored, though her hair is once again a glorious blonde, which must have done something to improve her mood. Tirini's skills in the sorcery of hair, clothes and jewellery are unmatched in the west. None of which will help us in the upcoming battle, but it does brighten the place up. The command tent is empty save for Makri who stands easily in the corner, a sword at each hip, watchful as always when she's on duty. Lisutaris lights a thazis stick. 'Thraxas, Bishop-General Ritari asked to speak to me in private.'

'About the war?'

'No, about you. He wanted to know if you were competent. Or, to be more accurate, if you were as incompetent as he's been led to believe.'

I let the insult pass. Niojans are always rude.

'The Bishop-General is anxious for us to make progress in identifying the murderer of Captain Istaros.'

'My unit is working on it full time. Didn't you tell me earlier not to bother you with any of this?'

'That was before the Bishop-General started harassing me. He's probably coming under pressure from his new Legate, Denpir. Captain Istaros was the King's nephew and Legate Denpir is the King's representative. As commander of the Niojan troops, it might look bad for the Bishop-General if the culprit isn't found.'

'Do we care if it looks bad for him?'

'As Niojans go, Ritari isn't the worst. He's not as hostile towards Turai as a lot of Niojans. Not as likely to declare war on us the moment the Orcs have departed. Turai is going to be vulnerable when this is all over, Thraxas. I'd rather Bishop-General Ritari was still in charge of their army when that happens, rather than some fanatic who might encourage their King to attack us while they have the chance.'

'Is the new Legate a fanatic?'

'Probably. He's a close ally of Archbishop Gudurius, head of the Niojan church.' Lisutaris finishes her thazis stick and lights another. 'I don't want Ritari made to look bad in front of their King. So start making some progress. That's an order.'

I scowl at our Commander. 'Before or after I wave my slate at the sky while being incinerated by a dragon?'

'If you wave your slate in unison with everyone else, you won't be incinerated. The sorcerous relay will work efficiently. As long as you're not too intoxicated, you'll be fine. Now kindly depart and solve the murder. Try not to implicate Ritari or any of his close associates.'

'What if they are implicated?'

'Find a more suitable candidate. Preferably someone we don't like.'

'I would never-'

'That will do, Captain Thraxas.' Lisutaris raises her hand. The tent flap swings open with the casual sort of sorcery she can do without even thinking about it. I depart, deep in thought. If I'm lucky, my unit will have made progress on the case. They've proved to be more competent than I expected. That's good, but it doesn't make me feel as positive as it might because thinking about my unit, I'm forced to acknowledge something I'd rather not: I don't entirely trust any of them. Anumaris Thunderbolt is intelligent and perceptive, but she's quite likely to be more loyal to Lisutaris and the Sorcerers Guild than she would be to me. As for Droo, she's trustworthy to an extent, though liable to let something slip while intoxicated. And what about the regular reports she's required to provide to the Elves? I can't risk any damaging information reaching the Elvish High Command. As for Rinderan, I've no reason to doubt him, but I've no particular reason to trust him either. The young sorcerer hails from the Southern Hills, a subject of Queen Direeva. What if he's sending reports of his activities back to her? Even if he's not, he's likely to show more loyalty to his guild than me. Lisutaris seems to have filled my security unit with people more loyal to her than me. Smart move on her part, I suppose.

I wonder if I should talk to Bishop-General Ritari. It's all very well for him to demand we find the culprit but it would be easier if his own Niojan troops were more co-operative. They haven't exactly been forthcoming with information. My thoughts turn to Makri and Magranos. That's an unwelcome complication. Major Magranos was killed in close proximity to Captain Istaros, and they were known to each other. The most likely explanation is that their deaths are linked, and nothing to do with Makri's desire for revenge on Magranos. Somehow I can't shake the feeling that Makri might be involved. It's the sort of thing she'd do. She didn't grow up with any notion of the due process of the law. There's no evidence against her but I'm worried Baron Vosanos might dig up something. I've instructed Droo to hang around the Samsarinans, to see what she can find out. Droo, a young and personable Elf, is welcome in most places. As I near the wagon, she stumbles into sight.

'Junior Ensign Sendroo, Elvish Reconnaissance Regiment, temporarily seconded to the Sorcerers Auxiliary Regiment, reporting on my investigations!'

She sits down heavily on a sack of rice. I raise my eyebrows. 'Did these investigation involve much wine?'

'No wine at all, Captain Thraxas. The Samsarinans just brought in a new wagon load of beer. I brought you a bottle.' Droo looks down at her hands. She's not carrying anything. 'No, I drank it on the way back.' Droo slides from the sack to the ground. Her eyes start to glaze over. At this moment, Anumaris Thunderbolt arrives.

'I've been talking to–' she pauses. 'What's wrong with Droo?'

'She's been investigating the Samsarinans.'

Droo rolls over on the ground and closes her eyes.

'Did she learn anything?'

'They have a new delivery of beer.'

'This is not satisfactory.' Anumaris looks at me as if it's my fault.

'She'll sleep it off, Anumaris.'

'It's a breach of discipline!'

'We don't know that. She might have been obliged to drink heavily while gathering information. It's often happened to me in the past.'

Anumaris is probably on the verge of pointing out that I set a bad example. To prevent this I ask her if she'd learned anything useful while out investigating.

'Not much,' she admits. 'I talked to several Niojan sorcerers. Major Stranachus had asked them about the possibility of investigating Legate Apiroi's death but an order arrived from Lisutaris forbidding all non-war related uses of sorcery, so that put an end to that.'

'Were they suspicious?'

'No. It's not an unusual order in wartime. It makes sense to conserve power. Is that really why Lisutaris issued the order?'

'I doubt it.'

'Do you think she's covering up her involvement?'

'Maybe.' Droo rolls over, settling her head comfortably on the sack of rice. Anumaris gives her another disapproving look. 'Here's Rinderan,' she says. 'Perhaps he's learned something.'

I sent Rinderan to talk to the Niojan soldiers, hoping he might learn something from those we weren't given access to earlier. Now that Bishop-General Ritari's expressed concern over the affair, it might have opened some doors. Rinderan steps nimbly over Droo's slumbering frame. He's young, still in good condition. The sorcerers of the Southern Hills are not as degenerate as our Turanians. 'I heard some interesting rumours from a sorcerer I knew back in the Southern Hills. She's been working with the Niojan Sorcerers Guild.'

'Why?'

'Queen Direeva likes her sorcerers to maintain good relations with other guilds, even the Niojans. According to my contact, the Bishop-General's been in dispute with the Niojan church. They've never got on, but recently it's been worse. She even thought that was why Ritari had recruited his special defence unit.'

'To protect him from the Niojan church?'

'So she said.'

'Could this have anything to do with Captain Istaros's death?'

'I couldn't find out anything more specific.'

'I thought it was the sorcerers that the Niojan church doesn't like,' says Anumaris. 'Don't they get on with the army either?'

'Who knows? The church in Nioj is so fanatical they probably hate everyone. If Captain Istaros was part of a unit whose task was to protect the Bishop-General from the Niojan church, and now he's dead, it might be connected. I wonder who can tell me anything about Niojan politics?'

Chapter Eight

Visiting Hanama in camp is not as unsettling as visiting her in the Assassins Guild headquarters in Turai but it's not something I relish. She might be wearing a uniform and a captain's insignia but she's still cold as an Orc's heart. I can't detect any signs of warmth or camaraderie between her and her intelligence unit. I doubt they sit around their fire at night drinking beer and swapping stories. Lisutaris thinks they're efficient: I have my doubts.

I'm expecting Hanama to be obstructive so I get to the point as swiftly and clearly as I can. 'Captain Hanama. I'm hoping you can tell me something about Niojan society.'

'What do you want to know?'

'Who has influence with the King?'

'Why do you want to know?'

I glare at her. 'Vital military work, so I'd appreciate it if you stopped being obstructive.'

Hanama regards me quite blankly. She doesn't have the most expressive face. It's never easy to tell what she's thinking.

'There are several strong factions in Nioj. The Legates lead the political class. They have allies at court among the aristocracy, and the support of landowners. They're closely allied to the Church. The Church has more power and wealth in Nioj than they do in other countries. So I'd say Legate Denpir and Archbishop Gudurius are the most powerful individuals, after the King. They consult with each other every day.'

'Archbishop Gudurius is here?'

'He joined the Niojan contingent last week.'

'Who are their rivals?'

'The army is the next most powerful force.'

'Is Bishop-General Ritari their most important figure?'

'Yes. He's unofficial leader of the army faction. That's a strong position, but he doesn't have as much influence at King Lamachus's court as the Legates and the church.'

'Any other factions?'

Hanama looks thoughtful. 'There's the Niojan Sorcerers Guild. They're rivals of the Church. More than rivals perhaps, because the

Church disapproves of them. However they're too important to the country to be got rid of. They have allies at court. Particularly Duchess Arbella. She owns a huge amount of land. She's probably the most influential woman in Nioj. The church doesn't like her either. She's a firm ally of the sorcerers. They're closer to General Ritari and the army than they are to the Legates or the Church.'

As I'm absorbing Hanama's information, several of her intelligence agents hover in the background, trying to look busy while listening in on our conversation.

'Thank you, Captain Hanama.' It takes an effort for me to say it.

'Presumably you think this may have some bearing on the death of Captain Istaros?'

'It might. There's no obvious criminal motive. I'm wondering if it might be part of some internal power struggle.'

'That would be unusual for Nioj.'

'Why? Wherever there's a King, there's a court full of jealous people, all trying to advance themselves.'

'True. However King Lamachus is known to be extremely strict about that sort of thing. Ever since rivalries got out of hand during his father's reign, vying for power in Lamachus's court is expressly forbidden. Anyone guilty of using underhand means to gain influence is liable to find himself exiled, or executed.'

'Interesting. Wouldn't stop it going on, I imagine.'

'Perhaps not,' agrees Hanama. 'If I learn anything useful, I'll let you know. Our Commander can't be distracted at this moment.'

I depart, heading for the Niojan encampment. I'm gathering momentum as I reach the their lines. If anyone tries getting in my way I'm going to mow them down. I've got a lot of weight and our War Leader on my side and I owe the Niojans a thing or two. At the perimeter of their encampment are two troopers and a sergeant. I march up to the sergeant. 'Captain Thraxas, head of our Commander's personal security unit. I'm here to investigate the death of Captain Istaros, and don't give me any of your Niojan runaround. I've had enough of you obstructive tactics. If you don't-'

The Niojan Sergeant salutes smartly. 'Bishop-General Ritari has been expecting you, Captain Thraxas.'

'He has?' I stand there foolishly for a moment. 'Are you sure?'

'He sent instructions to escort you to his tent the moment you arrived.'

'How did? Never mind. Take me there.'

Deflated by the Niojan's unexpected co-operation, I follow along as the sergeant leads me past the rows of small soldiers' tents towards the larger tents in the centre that house the senior officers. One is much larger than any other, tall, square and black, with a Niojan flag fluttering above it. The command centre of Bishop-General Ritari. I take a swift mental inventory, checking to see if I've actually insulted the Bishop-General in the past. Not that I can remember. A few comments perhaps, but nothing too outrageous. As for his feelings towards me, he did privately ask Lisutaris if I was competent, but I suppose that's not too antagonistic. Lisutaris regards him as not overly hostile to Turai so it's probably worth being polite to him, at least at first.

The Bishop-General is a man of medium build but wiry, with the look of an experienced soldier. He has scarring on his jaw, battle scars, most likely. He's clean-shaven and cropped-haired, like all Niojan officers. His black uniform is neater than might be expected given the action we've seen. His tent is tidier than our War Leader's. I find the neatness mildly irritating though that might just be because I'm looking for reasons not to like him. His greeting is not too unfriendly by Niojan standards. 'Captain Thraxas. I've been expecting you. These deaths need investigating.'

'Your officers haven't been that co-operative so far.'

'No military force is keen to have outsiders examining their affairs. I had hoped the death of Captain Istaros might be solved quickly by questioning my own officers. Unfortunately that hasn't happened. Therefore I welcome your investigation. I said as much to our War Leader only yesterday.'

Yesterday he was telling our War Leader I was an idiot. I let it pass. 'When you questioned your officers about Captain Istaros did you come up with anything?'

The Bishop-General shakes his head. 'Nothing that pointed towards any reason for murder. The Captain had no known enemies. I'm inclined to believe the attack came not from a Niojan, but an intruder.'

'That's possible. There was someone else in your encampment. Major Magranos, a Samsarinan. Unfortunately he's also dead.'

'Could he have killed Captain Istaros?'

'And then conveniently been killed right afterwards? It's unlikely. I'm wondering why none of your guards reported seeing Major Magranos entering your encampment.'

'Most of our security is targeted towards the outside perimeter. Keeping watch for the Orcs. Inside, with so many armies together, things are less disciplined, unfortunately perhaps.'

'Can you tell me anything about Major Magranos?'

'No. I was hoping you'd be able to enlighten me. Apart from learning he was involved in the purchase of land by Istaros in Samsarina, I know nothing about him. Do you?'

'I haven't learned anything significant,' I admit. 'The land deal seemed legitimate. Istaros wanted to build a house in Elath. He was the King's nephew, and a lot of important people own houses there because of the sword-fighting tournament.'

'The sword-fighting tournament.' A scowl passes over the Bishop-General's face. 'They tell me the Orcish woman won.'

'She did.'

'I find that difficult to believe. Though I understand there was outside interference.'

'You could say that. A dragon got in the way. But she'd have won it anyway.'

The Bishop-General doesn't look convinced. He lets it pass.

'Captain Thraxas, you seem to be searching for some motive for these killings. Is it not possible they were simply criminal acts? Robberies?'

'It's possible, though it doesn't seem likely. Murder and robbery aren't unknown among troops but rarely towards the climax of a campaign. We're almost at the walls of Turai. I just don't see any of your Niojan soldiers breaking discipline to do something like that.'

Ritari agrees with me. 'Even so, there are plenty of fellow travellers. Chefs, wagon drivers, metal-smiths, all sorts. No discipline among them.'

The Bishop-General is keen to push the idea that whoever murdered Captain Istaros, it wasn't a Niojan. I change tack. 'I understand there are several factions in Nioj, all competing for influence with the King. The legates, the church, the army and the sorcerers. With you being the head of one of those factions. Might the King's nephew have become caught up in some sort of power struggle?'

Ritari's tone hardens. He's not so friendly now. 'There are no factions in Nioj. Our society is united behind the King.'

'That's not the way I hear it.'

'You're on the wrong track. I don't know who's been telling you these things about Nioj, but really, there are no serious rivalries.' Ritari has already regained his polite demeanour. It's making me suspicious. No senior Niojan has ever made an effort to be polite to me before.

'I'll carry on investigating, Bishop-General. It will help if your Niojan troops are more co-operative.'

'They will be. I've given orders.'

I'm thoughtful as I leave the command tent. I haven't really learned anything but it was interesting the way the Bishop-General decided to be co-operative. Back at the wagon, Droo, Anumaris and Rinderan are waiting. 'Interesting news,' I tell them.

'What happened?'

'The Bishop-General was unusually polite and co-operative. Clearly he's up to something. Droo, find me a bottle of beer then everyone leave me alone while I think about things.'

Droo produces a bottle of beer apparently from nowhere. She stole it in readiness for me. She's an excellent soldier in every way. Unfortunately, as I'm clambering into the wagon, Major Stranachus arrives. I glare at the Niojan agent, at this moment about as welcome as an Orc at an Elvish wedding. 'Major Stranachus. I'd offer you beer but I need it all for myself.'

'I don't drink on duty,' says the Major, pleasantly. He's carrying a canvas bag, a military item with Niojan insignia. He reaches inside and pulls out a chainmail shirt. I recognise the shirt but don't let it show.

'I thought you might find this interesting. It belonged to Legate Apiroi. Part of his belongings we'll be sending back to his family after our investigation is finished.'

'Investigation?'

The major turns the mail shirt over. There's a sort of seam running down the back, made of links larger than the rest, the place where the shirt is joined together during the manufacturing process. He points to one of the links.

'You see this scratch?

I don't like the way this is going. 'What scratch?'

The major indicates a tiny mark on the edge of the metal link. 'Here.'

'What about it?'

'Could be a mark made by something passing through. A dart, for instance. Poisoned, perhaps.'

'A dart?' I scoff at the notion. 'No one could throw a dart through that tiny space.'

'An assassin might,' says the major. He looks at me. I look back at him. 'Have you come across any assassins in the army?'

'None that I know of,' I lie. 'No reason for any of them to be here.'

'You wouldn't have thought so.'

The Niojan still sounds affable. He's not fooling me with that any more. 'I doubt anyone threw a dart through Legate Apiroi's chainmail.'

The major looks down at the mail shirt. 'I'm sure you've come across highly accomplished assassins in your line of work. Turai has a large Assassins Guild. I was planning to ask our Niojan sorcerers to look back in time and see if they could cast any light on the murder. Unfortunately our War Leader has banned all uses of sorcery except for war purposes.'

'The Sorcerers Regiment needs to concentrate its power on the war effort. Can't be using sorcery for lighting camp fires.'

'Or solving inconvenient murders.'

I'm sick of Major Stranachus and want him to go away. He shows no signs of leaving. Maybe being rude would help. 'Did you just come here to waste my time with insinuations?'

'Just pointing out a few inconsistencies. You must admit, Legate Apiroi's death was suspicious.'

'Only to you.'

'I hear Lisutaris's bodyguard, Ensign Makri, is a suspect in Major Magranos' murder.'

'Idle gossip. The Samsarinan Baron Vosanos never liked her.'

'That doesn't seem enough reason to accuse her of murder.'

'What's it to you?' I say. 'Are you investigating that as well? Shouldn't you be concentrating on the King's dead nephew?'

'The murder of the Samsarinan major might be linked to that. Hard to tell what's linked. Anything might be.' He gazes at the mail shirt. 'Captain Istaros and Major Magranos did encounter some unpleasantness in Elath.'

'What happened?'

'Some sort of altercation. I don't know the details. I only heard about it because Captain Istaros arrived back from Elath earlier than expected. I was wondering if you might know more.'

'Why would I?'

'You were in Elath at the same time. You, your Orcish friend, Lisutaris and various other Turanians. It wouldn't be that surprising if some of them got into a fight with visiting Niojans.'

I don't deny it. There's no point pretending Turanians abroad are renowned for their good behaviour. 'No, it wouldn't be that surprising. However, I never heard anything about it.'

I sip from my bottle of beer. It's Simnian; not that good. They've never been great brewers. Major Stranachus takes another look at the chainmail he's holding, pointedly staring at the tiny scratch on the back.

'Is it true that Captain Hanama is a member of the Turanian Assassins Guild?'

I stare at the major. There's a lot of staring going on in this conversation. 'Not as far as I know.'

He smiles, knowing I'm lying. It's time to bring this conversation to an end before Stranachus embarrasses me further. Unable to think of any tactful way to get rid of the him, I ask him to leave. 'I have work to get on with. I really can't spare any more time. Thanks for your observations.'

The major nods politely. 'Please let me know if you discover anything relevant.' With that he departs, still affable. I'm starting to detest him. Major Stranachus and Niojan intelligence seem to know a lot about things I'd rather they didn't. All of my security unit have been listening surreptitiously to our conversation, as I'd expect them to do. Anumaris asks me if I knew anything about Captain Istaros having some sort of trouble in Elath.

'No. I didn't even know he was there. I was too busy guiding Makri to victory in the swordfighting tournament.'

'Why did Major Stranachus mention it?'

'I'm wondering that too. It doesn't seem to relate to anything here.'

'Makri was at the tournament and now she's a suspect for the murder of Major Magranos,' says Anumaris. 'Perhaps even Captain Istaros too.'

'Why would she be suspected of that?' asks Rinderan.

'Getting rid of a witness, perhaps?'

Rinderan frowns. 'Surely Ensign Makri wouldn't kill a man for that? Would she?' Rinderan looks at me. I decline to answer.

'Was Captain Hanama in Elath?' asks Anumaris.

'No.' I pause, thinking back. 'At least, I don't think so. She joined the army later, when we gathered outside the capital. I don't know where she was before that.'

'Does Captain Stranachus really suspect Captain Hanama of killing Legate Apiroi?'

'He might. Or he might have no idea what's been going on and is hoping he can just blame everything on Turanian assassins.

Rinderan drums his fingers on the side of the wagon. 'This all seems to have become more complicated.'

'That does tend to happen.' I shake my head, wearily. 'Our Commander wants this all to disappear without bothering her. With Major Stranachus poking around, that's not likely. I never expected the Niojans to have a smart investigator. It's annoying.' I yawn. 'I need to think. All three of you, talk to your contacts. Find out what happened to Captain Istaros in Elath. I want to know what trouble he was in.'

Chapter Nine

I finally mange to retreat to the wagon for a much needed rest. I'm slumbering peacefully when I'm abruptly awakened. I open my eyes to find Droo, Anumaris and Rinderan standing over me and a terrible cacophony blaring in the background. I have no idea what's happening.

'Captain, you have to get up!'

'Why?'

'Dragon attack!'

I shake my head to clear it. The noise in the background is the trumpets sounding the alarm.

'Your slate!' cries Anumaris.

'My what?'

'You have to take your position in the dragon shield.'

Cursing everything, particularly dragons, I haul myself upright and stumble from the wagon.

'Good luck,' says Anumaris. Having assured themselves that I'm awake and functioning, she and Rinderan depart briskly, heading for their allotted positions beneath the sorcerous dragon shied. The non-sorcerers who've been drafted in to help don't have allotted positions. We're just meant to stand in the open, holding up magic slates, while the sorcerers do the rest, relaying and amplifying their power through us. It's bound to end in disaster. I turn to Droo. 'This is bound to end in disaster.'

The sky is going dark with dragons, all diving towards the purple light which now covers our encampment in a great semi-circle overhead.

'You'll be fine,' says Droo. With that she disappears under the wagon, sensibly getting herself out of the way. I take a few paces till I'm standing in open ground, then raise the small piece of slate into the air and mutter the incantation that will bring it to life. A slight vibration runs through my fingers as it links with the other sorcerous items, boosting their power. As I raise my head the dragons are starting to hurtle themselves into the barrier. Now we're so close to Turai, Amrag has sent out a large force in an attempt to annihilate us. Flames crackle over the top of the shield as they attack. The sorcerous barrier repels the flames but as the huge beasts crash into it, the earth shakes. I can feel the force of their attack pummelling me from above. I knew this would happen. You can't wave a magic slate at dragons without suffering the consequences. Not far from me, a man in a butcher's apron, another hapless recruit to this foolish enterprise, buckles at the knees. As two huge dragons slam into the barrier directly overhead, he falls to the ground, still waving his slate but unable to rise. I stagger backwards under the pressure but manage to stay upright.

'You're doing well, Captain Thraxas,' calls Droo encouragingly, from beneath the wagon. I can't see any other slate bearers apart from me and the butcher. Nor can I see any sorcerers. By now they should be distributed evenly around our encampment but none of them have appeared in my vicinity. 'Dammit, am I meant to do this all myself!' I roar, and wave my slate defiantly at the sky. Another enormous dragon slams in the shield. The shock sends me to my knees, almost numbing my arm. I scramble back to my feet, shaking my other fist. 'Come down here and try that! I'll send you back where you came from!'

'That's the spirit!' cries Droo. 'Don't give in.'

The unfortunate man in the butcher's apron has now passed out. His slate lies beside him on the ground, no longer assisting our defences. The dragon overhead rises, shoots flames at the shield, then dives to attack again. As if sensing some weakening of the barrier, another great beast rushes to join it. I brace myself and hope that the sorcerous power currently being funnelled into my talisman is operating at full power, because if it's not, I'm going to be buried under two large dragons. As they crash into the barrier the very air seems to bend. The shield is pushed downwards through the sky and the colour fades as if stretched and weakened. A shockwave travels from the slate down my frame. My legs buckle and I tumble to the ground.

'Where are the sorcerers!' I scream. 'Cowards, all of them!'

The two dragons continue their attack and the sorcerous shield dips lower and lower, a depression that's coming nearer and nearer. I can see the bestial rage on the dragons' faces as they force their way towards me, hurtling themselves again and again against the obstruction. I'm unable to rise. I can barely hold my slate in the air. I'm going to die here, victim of the poor planning of our useless War Leader Lisutaris and her equally useless Sorcerers Regiment.

'Captain Thraxas, that's not the recommended position for sorcerous slate manipulation.'

I find myself grabbed by several pairs of hands and hauled upright. Four sorcerers in rainbow cloaks have arrived: Sareepa Lightning Strikes the Mountain and three of her Matteshan companions. Sareepa grins. 'You're not meant to roll around on the grass.'

'Damn you sorcerers! Am I meant to fight them off on my own?'

Already Sareepa's companions are pointing towards the sky. I watch as their power repels the creatures above, forcing the shield upwards. The downward bulge disappears and the barrier returns to its proper shape. Both dragons continue their attack but are unable to make an impression on the now-strengthened magical shield. As I watch, they begin to tire. Their great wings beat more slowly and fire no longer emerges from their mouths. For the first time I'm able to survey the whole sky overhead. Everywhere the same phenomenon can be seen. The fury of the attack is fading. Our sorcerers have held them off. I feel my own strength returning. I glare at Sareepa. 'Nice work. Maybe next time you could help me before I'm battered half to death.'

Sareepa laughs, very inappropriately. 'We had a lot to do elsewhere. Huge attack at our Commanders tent, took a lot of power to repel it.'

'You were protecting the most powerful sorcerer in the west? While hapless assistants were left on their own?'

Sareepa's still smiling, apparently finding the whole thing amusing. 'Of course. She's much more important than you. Anyway, you survived, didn't you? I knew you'd be fine, Thraxas.'

The butcher is slowly climbing to his feet, still looking dazed. One of the Matteshan sorcerers assists him, checking he's all right and his slate is undamaged. Sareepa herself appears invigorated, as if she enjoyed the battle. Perhaps she did. She always was up for a fight. Overhead the dragons are spiralling upwards and heading east. The barrier glows brightly, still a strong protection.

'Let's go,' Sareepa says to her sorcerers. 'See if anyone else needs help. Some of these volunteers haven't got Captain Thraxas's strength.'

I glare at her, not sure if she's being sarcastic or not. 'Next time get here quicker.'

'Stop complaining, Thraxas. I'll bring you some beer tonight. Good Matteshan ale, better than your Turanian rubbish.'

I'm about to respond, defending the integrity of Turanian beer, but I'm too drained to come up with anything witty so I let it go. Sareepa Lightning Strikes the mountain strides off, leading her sorcerers away. I limp slowly back towards the wagon. Droo crawls out from underneath.

'Do you have any–'

The young Elf hands me an open bottle of wine before I finish my sentence. I take a long drink. 'Useless sorcerers. Letting me get battered like that while they all huddled in safety with Lisutaris.'

'You did well,' says Droo, brightly. 'You hardly got thrown to the ground at all. Only a few times. Much better than that other man in the apron, he was hopeless.'

I nod. 'He was. Of course, he didn't have my experience. I still know a few things about sorcery. Takes intelligence to make it work. Strength as well. Not many men could have stood up to that onslaught. These were big dragons I was holding off. Lucky I was in position or we might be in a lot of trouble.' I drink more wine. A wave of fatigue washes over me. I tell Ensign Droo I'm heading inside the wagon to rest, and instruct her to keep everyone away from me.

'Will do. You'll need some rest before your tryst.'

'Tryst? What tryst?'

'With Sareepa Lightning Strikes the Mountain.'

'I don't have a tryst with Sareepa.'

'Yes you do,' says Droo. 'I heard her say she was coming over to visit you with beer.'

'That's not a tryst. That's drinking beer.'

'It sounded like an tryst to me.'

'Trysts are secret meetings between lovers!'

'Well, she didn't know I was listening,' says Droo.

I shake my head. 'Stop being ridiculous. And stop saying *tryst*. It's starting to make my head hurt.' I depart into the wagon before I have to listen any more foolishness from Droo. Once inside, I lay down, rest my head on a bag for a pillow, and fall asleep, a sleep I'm entitled to after defending the armies of the west against such a major dragon attack. Not many men could have stood up to it, you can be certain of that.

Chapter Ten

I slumber peacefully before being wakened by raised voices outside the wagon.

'What do you mean *don't wake him*? We need to wake him.' It's Anumaris Thunderbolt.

Droo replies. 'Captain Thraxas had a hard struggle against the dragons. They kept knocking him over. We should let him rest.'

'Was he injured?'

'Not seriously. But he didn't look too good afterwards.'

'We need to wake him,' comes Rinderan's voice. 'We have to report.'

Droo refuses to be overruled. 'Let him rest. He was really pummelled by these dragons. There were a lot of heavy blows.'

While I'm not pleased at Droo's exaggeration of the pummelling I received, I do appreciate the positive report she's giving of my performance. At least one member of my security unit respects me.

'We were attacked too,' says Anumaris. 'But we're back on duty now. I really think we should be reporting to our unit commander.'

'Thraxas needs his sleep!' insists Droo.

I'm warming to the young Elf more and more.

'He has a tryst with Sareepa later so he'll need to be well-rested.'

I find myself clutching my brow and wondering how I ended up in the same unit as the idiotic young Elf. This has gone far enough. I poke my head out of the wagon to find Anumaris and Rinderan regarding me with an unusual degree of interest.

'Captain Thraxas...' There's an odd tone in Anumaris's voice. 'Sorry if we woke you. You should be...resting.'

I clamber out of the wagon. 'I'm fine.'

'We can come back later,' says Rinderan. 'Really, there's no urgency. Droo tells us you need to rest because...' His voice tails off, but his smile shows what he's thinking.

I give Droo a hostile glance. 'Would you stop telling people I'm having some sort of secret romance?'

'A romance?' exclaims Anumaris. 'I didn't realise it had gone that far.'

'I congratulate you,' says Rinderan. 'Sareepa is a fine woman and a credit to the Matteshan Sorcerers Guild.'

My unit has apparently gone insane. It's time to put a stop to this nonsense. 'There is no romance. Ensign Sendroo is imagining things. Now make your report on the dragon attack and any associated problems.'

'I didn't say it was a romance,' protests the young Elf. 'Just a tryst.' She looks thoughtful. 'I suppose the romance would come later. Happens a lot in our epic poetry. I suppose it's the danger and excitement of war.'

I give her the most hostile glare I can manage. 'There is no tryst. And I told you to stop saying that word.'

'Would *assignation* be better?' Droo turns to Anumaris. 'If people made a secret arrangement to drink beer at night would that be a tryst or an assignation?'

'They seem to mean much the same thing.' Anumaris turns to me. 'Not that I would interfere, Captain Thraxas, but is this wise? We'll be in battle any day now.'

'That's no reason to hold back,' says Rinderan. 'We could all be dead soon. If Captain Thraxas can obtain some happiness with Sareepa, I'd say he should grasp the opportunity.'

'Will you all-'

I'm interrupted by Droo. 'Here's Makri. She's good with language. Makri, would you say a secret meeting with lovers and beer is a tryst or an assignation?'

Maki halts, a look of surprise on her face. 'Which lovers are meeting in secret?'

'Thraxas and Sareepa Lightning Strikes the Mountain.'

'What? When did this happen?'

'During the dragon attack,' says Droo.

Makri looks at me. 'Weren't you mean to be repelling dragons?'

'I was repelling dragons.'

'Then how did you find time to arrange an assignation with Sareepa? You can't have been doing much repelling.'

I raise my voice. 'Everyone be quiet! Stop talking about trysts, assignations and romance. There is no tryst, assignation or romance. Sareepa simply mentioned she'd bring me some beer, a richly deserved reward for my heroic actions in the recent dragon attack.' I glare at Makri. 'During which I did plenty of repelling. And now, having cleared up a matter which was no concern of any of you in the first place, I intend to eat. Is that clear?'

Anumaris raises her eyebrows a fraction. 'Yes, Captain. But we really do need to report to you.'

'And I have an important matter to discuss,' says Makri.

'Fine. Report and discuss as you please. But no more talk of assignations.'

I walk towards the fire, the embers of which are still smouldering. Now that Lisutaris has banned all extraneous sorcery, it's annoying and inconvenient if the fire goes out, requiring a lot of messing around with tinder boxes to light it again. I eat the standard military meal with my unit. A small portion of salted beef, yams which are none too fresh, and the flat, sweetened oatcakes which are ubiquitous among the Turanian army. None of it terrible but none of it satisfying. I've eaten enough of these rations during my life to be used to them but I'll be heading over to Tanrose's campfire at the earliest opportunity to top up with better food. Anumaris and Rinderan tell us of their experiences during the dragon raid. Both used their sorcery to support the shield. Neither were injured and neither felt that the shield was about to break, though I can tell from their voices they have some doubts.

'Don't you think we can keep it up?'

'Probably,' says Anumaris.

'Maybe,' says Rinderan.

'That's not a resounding vote of confidence.' I hunt around for more salted beef but there's none. Army rations, they're really not satisfying.

'The shield did work well enough,' says Rinderan. 'But we were stretched thin. There were weak spots. We managed to cover them this time but some sorcerers are worried.'

'Is this going to be a problem?'

'I'm sure we can cope,' says Anumaris.

Rinderan chuckles. 'Anumaris isn't going cast any doubts on Lisutaris. She's too loyal.'

Anumaris doesn't comment. I ask Rinderan to elaborate.

'We're only just managing to repel these dragons. The closer we get to Turai the more difficult it's going to be. When we're camped next to the city the Orcish sorcerers will be able to attack the barrier with all their power. With the dragons attacking too, it's going to be difficult. That's before we even start thinking about the trench. Protecting that is going to take a lot of power. The sorcerers providing that power won't be able to help with the overhead barrier. I can see it going wrong.'

'What about that calculating sorcerer, Dearineth the Precise Measurer? She said we had an advantage of two points in three hundred or something like that. Was she just making that up?'

Rinderan shrugs. 'Dearineth has a good reputation. She's specialised in measuring in a way no one's done before. But two points in three hundred, in a calculation of sorcerous power? We're not even certain how many Orcish sorcerers there are. And dragons interfere with sorcery, so I'm not even sure how Dearineth managed to include them in her measurements. I can see plenty of room for error. So can others, though they're not going to come right out and say it. No one wants to appear disloyal to Lisutaris.'

I gaze at my empty plate. Army rations aren't designed for a man of my appetites. No wonder I'm losing weight. 'Makri, what do you think about all this?'

'I have complete confidence in Lisutaris.'

I can tell she's having doubts too. 'Anumaris, what was it you needed to report to me?'

'When Captain Istaros was in Elath, there was some trouble, and it was more than just an argument. Someone was killed.'

'Really? Who told you this?'

'A Turanian who was there, a young merchant's assistant. He was walking from one tavern to the next when he saw a swordfight in the street, with four or five people involved. He saw someone he thought was Captain Istaros cutting down one of his opponents. Then everyone fled.'

'He never reported any of this before?'

'No.'

'Was he questioned by the Guards in Elath?'

'No. He slipped away before anyone saw him'

'Who is this elusive character and how do you know him?'

Anumaris looks embarrassed. 'I promised not to reveal his name. He's a thazis supplier. I've encountered him once or twice ...'

'Meaning he supplies thazis to Lisutaris?'

'To unspecified people, possibly sorcerers.'

I laugh. 'Our War Leader needs a regular supply now she's away from her own garden. Good work, Anumaris. So Captain Istaros actually killed someone in Elath. If we can find out more about the fight it'll take us a long way forward.'

'The man who was killed was wearing some sort of distinctive hat. A green cap. From the description, it sounded like the sort of thing religious assistants wear in Nioj.'

Again, this is interesting news. 'If Istaros was in a fight with people from the Niojan church it does suggest this is part of some power struggle.'

'Is that good or bad?' asks Droo.

'I don't know. At least it doesn't involve Bishop-General Ritari so far. It might lead to him, which would be bad.'

Makri has been quiet. I can tell she's disgruntled about something or other. She picks at her food without much enthusiasm. She's never been a big eater anyway. I've often told her she'd be a lot better off with a few hearty meals inside her but she doesn't listen. Later I walk back with her towards her tent. 'What did you want to discuss?'

'If something bad happened, for instance an innocent mathematical mistake causing a massive death toll and the defeat of the west, do you think people would remember who was responsible?'

I come to a halt. 'I take it the calculations are still going badly?'

'Very badly,' says Makri. 'It's worrying. I don't want to be remembered as the person who caused everything to go wrong! If I end up the villain in an epic poem it will be really unfair.'

'Villain in an epic poem? That doesn't seem likely.'

Makri raises her voice. 'It happens! The Elves have a whole cycle of poems about the war and misery caused by Bar-ir-Lith the weaver when he stole sheep from Lord Diras. Generations of Elves were massacred because of it. Bar-ir-Lith comes out of it all very badly. But it's not really clear, historically speaking, that it was his fault at all. They could have been his sheep all along.'

My head swims, as sometimes happens when talking to Makri. 'I really don't think epic poetry is your main concern at the moment. Anyway, if everything goes wrong there won't be anyone left to write about you.'

'Some Elvish bards can survive anything.' Makri scowls. 'They'd like nothing better than to blame a woman with Orcish blood for the destruction of the west. I can hear them sharpening their quills already.'

Makri's hair is long, thick and unruly at the best of times but since being appointed as Lisutaris's bodyguard she's made an effort to keep it in check, tying it back neatly while in uniform. These efforts now seem to be failing, as strands break free from captivity and blow around her face in the breeze. It's time to speak firmly. 'Makri, desist with these delusions. And cut down on your intake of Lisutaris's extra-strong thazis. You're not going to end up the villain in an Elvish epic. Concentrate on the work in hand. Is the mathematics still incomprehensible?'

Makri shudders. 'It's getting worse. Arichdamis invented another new dimension. I was just getting the hang of how we get the sorcery into the third new dimension and thinking about how it might progress to the fourth. And now he's just decided there's a fifth new dimension and we have to calculate for it as well!' Makri looks cross. 'I don't like it. It's not proper mathematics. You can't just go around inventing new dimensions every time you have a problem.' Her shoulders slump. 'Except you can if you're Arichdamis. His mathematical powers are incredible. I can sometimes almost understand it when he's explaining it to me but afterwards it's just too complex to engage with. I'm lost. If it comes down to me having to do any of his mathematics, we're doomed. The Orcs won't even have to do anything. I'll send our own sorcery up the wrong path and it will kill everyone in our army.'

'What about the Lezunda Blue Glow?'

'He's all right, I suppose. Seems to understand it well enough.' Makri scowls again, still not liking it that there's another person smarter than her.

'At least there are two of them doing the work. Providing they don't both drop dead all you need to do is check their figures. Is there any chance they're wrong?'

'I don't know,' admits Makri. 'I have confidence in Arichdamis but not everyone does. You remember that Simnian sorcerer, Gorsoman? The one who was complaining about Arichdamis using untested formulae? He's still complaining about it. Not too loudly, in case Lisutaris slaps him down, but there are whispers among the other sorcerers that Arichdamis doesn't know what he's doing.'

We come to a halt near Makri's small tent, close to Lisutaris's command centre. The sky above is dark and clear, with two moons visible. Both are on the wane. The nights will be darker when we reach Turai. 'Warfare used to be simpler. You marched towards your opponents and the strongest army won. Or the bravest. Didn't used to involve a lot of calculations. I don't like it.' I sigh. 'Well, I didn't expect to come out of this alive anyway.'

A new tent has appeared close to Lisutaris's. It's larger than those used by the common soldiers, larger even than those belonging to our generals and senior sorcerers. It belongs to Tirini Snake Smiter. Now she's back to health, Lisutaris has positioned her nearby. Tirini Snake Smiter isn't the sort of person who's going to sit through tedious strategy meetings but she's very powerful and our War Leader trusts her. She's an old friend of Lisutaris's, maybe her oldest friend. As far as I can gather, her task is to remain close to our Commander, providing her with extra sorcerous protection. I don't know what her role will be when we reach Turai. I can't see her storming the walls in her high heels and fancy dresses, but perhaps she'll surprise us.

Makri is equivocal about Tirini's elevation. 'She's not reliable. Yesterday Lisutaris told me I could take a break from bodyguarding and I didn't want to but she said it was fine because Tirini was there.' Makri frowns. 'I didn't think that was a great idea. When I got back she was trying on a new dress. She told me she was keeping an eye on Lisutaris at the same time but I didn't believe her. Lisutaris shouldn't be depending on her.'

Makri's right, though some of her objections might be down to professional jealousy. Makri likes her position as bodyguard and takes it seriously. She's sensitive to anyone trying to usurp her.

'She wasn't even happy with the dress! She'd worked spells on it but it still wasn't good enough. Now she's complaining about having to walk round the camp like a common fisherwoman even though she used a spell to make her shoes silver and another one to get her hair right.'

'I noticed it was looking very blonde.'

Makri shakes her head. 'I really don't think she's reliable for bodyguard duties.'

As evening turns into night it's peaceful. Earlier in our march the army encampment was prone to wild outbursts, raucous behaviour from soldiers, but that's not happening now. Nearing the enemy, everything feels more serious.

'Are you really having a tryst with Sareepa?'

'No. She said she'd being me some beer. Droo heard her and got carried away.' I pause. 'I don't like the thought of Droo dying outside the walls of Turai. She's just a young Elvish poet, when it comes right down to it. She shouldn't be here.'

'You could say that about a lot of people.' Makri looks towards our Commander's tent. 'This wasn't what I had in mind when I came to Turai. I wanted to see civilisation. I wanted to study. I thought I was done with Orcs. I wasn't expecting to be involved in a war.' She shrugs. 'Not that I really mind.'

Makri asks me how things are with my investigation. I tell her I've made some progress with the murder of Captain Istaros, but none with the murder of Major Magranos.

'Have you really made no progress or are you just not telling me about it because I'm a suspect?'

'I've really made no progress.'

'Right. I notice you didn't contradict me when I said I was a suspect.'

It's my turn to shrug. 'We haven't found anyone with a better motive.'

'Have you found anyone with a motive for anything?'

'Not really. There's some internal trouble between Niojans but I've no idea how Magranos might be connected. Unless he just got himself killed because he saw what happened to Captain Istaros.'

Makri looks at me suspiciously. 'Am I suspected of his murder too?'

'That depends. Would you get rid of a witness?'

'Probably, if I had to. But I had nothing to do with any of this.'

'It would help if I could at least find another suspect.'

'How hard have you been looking?'

'My unit has been doing most of the work. If it wasn't for Anumaris I probably wouldn't have learned anything at all. It's my fault. I haven't been able to concentrate on the investigation.'

There's a silence.

'But?' says Makri.

'But what?'

'Usually you'd finish that sentence with some excuse. Like "*I haven't been able to concentrate on the investigation because of my heroic work on the battlefield.*"'

'I don't have an excuse.'

'So what's the problem?' asks Makri.

'I don't know. My investigating powers seem to have disappeared.'

I trudge off towards my wagon. I hope Sareepa is bringing me good beer. I could do with it.

Chapter Eleven

Sareepa is waiting outside my tent. She doesn't appear to be carrying any beer. 'Thraxas, where have you been? I've been waiting for you.'

'No beer?' I scan her figure, hoping she might have secreted some bottles in a magic pocket. 'Is it hidden somewhere?'

'Never mind beer,' says Sareepa.

'What do you *mean never mind beer*? You're not making sense.'

Sareepa climbs swiftly into the wagon and motions for me to follow. Puzzled, and prepared to be mightily disappointed, I follow her inside. The interior of the wagon is lit by the gentle glow of an illuminated staff that makes it easy to see the semi-conscious figure of Lisutaris, Mistress of the Sky, lying on the floor.

'What's going on?'

'A great excess of thazis.' Sareepa looks grim. 'She's meant to be at a meeting with her officers. Tirini is stalling them. We can't let them see her like this.'

'So you brought her here?'

'Where else? It took a lot of sneaking around with concealment spells to get here. You're experienced in this, I believe?'

I have, in the past, been witness to episodes of extreme thazis intoxication on the part of Lisutaris. If I hadn't covered up for her in Turai she'd never have been made Head of the Sorcerers Guild. If I hadn't covered up for her in Samsarina she'd never have been made War Leader. Maybe covering up for her wasn't such a great idea. It's too late to worry about that now.

'Do what you can,' says Sareepa. 'I have to go and help Tirini. She's probably talking to the generals about her shoes and that's not going to hold their attention for long.' Sareepa departs briskly, leaving behind her illuminated staff. I look down at Lisutaris. Her face is pale and her hair is dishevelled, long brown strands matted across her face. Her cloak is dusty, as if it's been in contact with the ground between her command tent and my wagon.

'Do you want to sit up or would you rather just lie there?'

Lisutaris doesn't reply. I have a small bag of personal supplies in the wagon. I reach inside and take out a lesada leaf. These leaves are excellent for hangovers and good against overdoses of dwa. They're not as effective for thazis, the intoxication being somewhat different, but they can clear the worst excesses. I help our Commander to sit up, then tear the leaf into small pieces, dump them in a jar of water, and pour it into her mouth. It's a messy process and it strikes me that if Lisutaris's senior officers were to see her at this moment, her role as War Leader would be brought to a swift end. Bishop-General Ritari and his Niojan regiments would depart, citing the impossibility of following a Commander who was a hopeless drug abuser, and also female, both things being unacceptable to their way of thinking.

'Lisutaris,' I say, quite sternly, neglecting to call her Commander. 'This is not acceptable behaviour.'

Lisutaris looks at me dully. 'That's rich, coming from you.' Her voice is unsteady, quite unlike the normal intonation of an aristocratic Turanian lady. Her head droops and she doesn't speak again for a while. I hope Sareepa and Tirini are doing a good job distracting the command council because our War Leader won't be appearing there any time soon. Outside, the encampment is still quiet. Finally the lesada leaf starts to take effect. I give Lisutaris more water and help her onto the bench at the side of the wagon. Colour returns to her face.

'What do you think you're doing?' I demand, forgoing any attempt at tact. 'Do you want the Niojans to depart? If you mess things up as War Leader we'll never get Turai back.'

'Stop exaggerating,' replies Lisutaris, waving her hand in the air. 'It's not like you ever made it through a day sober.'

'I'm not Commander of the western forces, you are. If you become incapacitated it could bring down nations. It's not acceptable behaviour and if it happens again I'll inform your command council.'

Angered, Lisutaris leaps to her feet and raises her hand imperiously. If she's about to cast a spell I doubt my spell-protection necklace will repel it. I've seen Lisutaris bring down two dragons with sorcery that seemed to rip apart the very fabric of reality. Whether she would actually fire a spell at me I don't find out, because her legs buckle under her. Having leapt up rather too, she now sinks to the floor. 'Oh dammit,' she mutters. 'Help me up.'

I help her back onto the bench. She looks miserable. 'I suppose it was irresponsible.'

'What happened? You're usually more in control.'

'My thazis tasted strange.'

'Strange? Some sort of poison?'

'No, not poison. Just the effects of one of the spells I use to make it stronger. It can happen sometimes that it makes a batch go bad. So I thought I'd better try some more.'

'Why?'

'To see if it had gone bad, of course. I couldn't quite make up my mind.'

'So you tried more?'

'Yes. Turned out it hadn't gone bad at all. But it had become stronger. Then I forgot what I was meant to be doing.' The sorceress takes an empty embroidered pouch from inside her cloak. 'Apparently I finished the whole bag. I don't remember that. Then I found myself lying on the grass. How did I get here?'

'Sareepa brought you.'

'Sareepa? I can't remember meeting her.'

'I'm not surprised. You've ingested enough enhanced thazis to levitate a dragon.'

'Dragons don't need levitation. They can fly.'

'Yes, it was a poor example. I was just thinking of a large animal. You get my point. You really can't do this again.'

Lisutaris sighs. 'I know. I'm sorry it happened.' She sits in silence for a while, recovering her strength. 'You wouldn't really have reported me to the council, would you?'

'Of course not. I was just trying to shake you up.'

'Could you bring me a glass of water? You know Thraxas, despite my admitted shortcomings, it's a bit much for you to get upset at anyone for being intoxicated.'

'Maybe.'

'Especially someone who saved your life during the war.'

I'm puzzled by this. 'I don't remember you saving my life. I do remember us heroically fighting off an army of Orcs.'

'We did, didn't we?' Lisutaris smiles at the memory. 'When I'd used up all my spells I picked up a broken sword and stood beside you and we hewed at them as they came over the walls. That was quite an experience. But I did save your life.'

'How?'

'When the wall collapsed. By then I'd recharged enough for one desperate spell. I used it to protect us from the rubble. I shielded you as we went down.'

I raise my eyebrows. 'I can't recall feeling any magic.'

'How could you? There was sorcery all over the place and dragons everywhere. You wouldn't have felt anything from my spell. But the fact is, I brought us out of that safely.'

I'm dubious. 'You never mentioned it before.'

'Well, one doesn't like to brag,' says Lisutaris, airily. 'No need for you to feel any sort of permanent obligation to me for saving your life. But you might remember it next time you go around creating a fuss over what was, when it comes right down to it, no more than a minor incident with a few enhanced thazis sticks. Nothing to get too upset about. Have you brought me a glass of water yet? I do have a terrible thirst.'

Lisutaris sips her water.

'If you're feeling better you should get back to your command council.

Our War Leader shrugs. 'There's no rush. Either Sareepa and Tirini have come up with a convincing explanation for my absence or they haven't. Tirini probably has, she's covered for me before.' Lisutaris looks at me. 'I suppose I owe you an apology over Sareepa.'

'What? Why?'

'For getting in the way. It was fortunate she found me and brought me here in secret, but it did rather ruin your assignation.'

'There was no assignation! Sareepa just said she'd bring me some beer and the impressionable female contingent of my security unit got carried away. That's what happens when you surround a fighting man like myself with a lot of women. I knew it would lead to trouble. No wonder I can't get anywhere with my investigations when my entire unit spends its time gossiping.'

Lisutaris laughs, rather coldly. 'From what I hear, the only information you've gathered has come from Anumaris doing her job properly.' Lisutaris looks closely at me. 'Is that true?'

I hesitate, wondering whether or not to lie. Then I shrug. 'It's fairly true. I haven't made as much progress as I should. I don't know why. The distractions...the war...I don't know, something's wrong.'

'Whatever's wrong, fix it. Bishop-General Ritari's becoming more annoyed all the time. The new Niojan Legate is just as bad. He's been hinting that we're not investigating the murders thoroughly enough because Istaros was Niojan. You know how eager they are to take offence.'

'Talking of Niojan Legates, did you have the last one killed?'

It's my turn to look Lisutaris in the eye and her turn to shrug. 'I gave the order. It seemed like the best way to deal with the problem. Can't say I regret it, he was an almighty nuisance and he was threatening to blackmail me.'

'He was, but–'

'So just make sure no one learns of it,' continues Lisutaris blithely. She yawns. 'I don't feel like talking to my officers right now. Is that a blanket over there? Do you have anything for a pillow?'

I hand her the soft bag I was using earlier. Lisutaris, Mistress of the Sky, War Leader and Head of the Sorcerers Guild, takes the pillow and the blanket, stretches out on the bench and goes to sleep. I've been sleeping in the wagon myself most nights but I'm now obliged to head outside to my small tent, reflecting on the odd circumstance that this is not the first time I've been obliged to give up my bed for Lisutaris. Last winter in Turai she fell victim to the malady while at the Avenging Axe. She spent a week recovering in my bedroom, cared for by sorcerers and healers, while I was banished to a remote part of the tavern. I couldn't even sleep in my office, it being occupied by a sick Hanama at the time. A sick Sarin the Merciless too. I wonder what became of that notorious criminal? I doubt she died when Turai fell. She'll have sneaked off somewhere.

I wrap myself up in my army-issue blanket. I'm dissatisfied with the way the evening went, principally because the promised beer didn't arrive. I'm dissatisfied with Lisutaris's behaviour too, but if she decides to endanger her position as War Leader by over-indulging in thazis I suppose that's her affair. Nothing I can do to prevent her. It's interesting that she came right out and admitted ordering Legate Apiroi's killing. Was she still feeling the effects of the thazis when she said that? Possibly. Otherwise why tell me? She'd know I'd disapprove. Not that it would worry her, I suppose. If Lisutaris saw getting rid of Legate Apiroi as necessary for the war effort, she wouldn't care if I approved or not. She'd know I wasn't going to tell anyone. *Our War Leader knows I'm loyal enough to cover up a murder.* That doesn't make me feel great. I drift off to sleep, not satisfied with anything. The sooner we reach the walls of Turai the better. I won't have to think about investigating any more.

Chapter Twelve

Having fallen asleep early and sober, I waken feeling unusually refreshed. The military camp is starting to come to life. When I emerge from my tent I glance over at the wagon, wondering if Lisutaris is still inside. Should I check on her? I'm undecided when I'm surprised by the appearance of Rinderan, Anumaris and Droo, all in uniform.

'Captain Thraxas!' exclaims Anumaris. 'I wasn't expecting you to be up at this hour.'

It's a fair point. I don't dispute it. 'Where have you been?'

'Investigating!' exclaims Droo.

The young Elf is excited, which worries me. 'Investigating what?'

'Captain Istaros, and why he went to Elath.'

'It struck us that it was worth checking,' explains Anumaris. 'Captain Istaros was said to have met Major Magranos in Elath while negotiating a land purchase from Baron Vosanos. I wondered if that were true. Istaros was an important man in Nioj, the King's nephew. Wouldn't he have been likely to send representatives to make the purchase on his behalf?'

'Did you learn anything?'

'Yes!' says Droo, happily. 'Anumaris is really good at investigating!'

'The assistant to the land registrar in Elath is here with the Samsarinan troops,' continues Anumaris. 'He was drafted into their army as a supply clerk. We went to talk to him in private.'

'We bribed him!' enthuses Droo, who's pleased to have been involved in anything shady.

Anumaris looks embarrassed.

'Bribery is fine,' I assure her.

'According to the land registrar's assistant, no transaction was made. He had no record of Istaros buying land from Baron Vosanos.'

'How reliable is that information?'

Anumaris ponders briefly. 'Reliable, I think. Elath isn't a large town. It's only busy during the tournament. The land registrar does record all transactions. If Istaros had bought land from the Baron, I can't see any reason it wouldn't have been recorded.'

'There are plenty of reasons it might not have been recorded. Tax, inheritance, secret trade deals, business rivalries, jealous family members - rich people move their assets around all the time and try to keep it from the authorities. '

Anumaris immediately looks deflated, as do Droo and Rinderan.

'Nonetheless it's good information. If it's true it means the land transaction may only have been an excuse for Captain Istaros to be in Elath. Good work, all of you.'

My unit are cheered. It was good work. It showed more initiative than I've managed recently.

'We should follow this up¬–' I begin, but I'm interrupted by the sound of Lisutaris emerging from the wagon behind us. She's yawning, while simultaneously fastening the top of her shirt and pulling on her cloak. She descends gracefully onto the grass.

'Morning, Captain Thraxas.' She smiles. 'I feel refreshed. Your wagon is more comfortable than I'd have expected. Well, I'd better get back to headquarters. I'd like you to visit me after breakfast. If my officers missed me last night, I might need your talent for lying to cover for me.'

With that, our Commander strolls off. I turn round to find my unit staring at me, wide-eyed. Or rather, Rinderan and Droo are staring at me. Anumaris seems fascinated by her feet.

'This is a surprise,' says Droo, the most tactless of Elves. 'Are you with Lisutaris now? Why did you change you mind? What was wrong with Sareepa?'

'I did not–'

'Our Commander is a fine-looking woman,' says Rinderan. 'I can understand it.'

'Won't Sareepa be insulted?'

Rinderan frowns. 'She might be. Captain Thraxas, is this wise? They're both very powerful sorcerers. If they get upset, you could be in trouble.'

Droo nods in agreement. 'Sorcerers can be very temperamental.'

'It looks like Makri was wrong,' says Rinderan.

'Makri? What did Makri say?' I demand.

Droo grins. 'She said you'd never go for an intelligent woman like Sareepa. According to Makri you'd be more likely to chase some lusty wench from the theatre.'

'*Lusty wench*? She said that?'

'Yes, those were her words. But then she said that actresses weren't usually good cooks so they wouldn't be able to make you enough pies, and that was probably why you're always single.'

I draw myself up. 'Enough of this nonsense. There has been no–'

At this moment a deafening racket breaks out as the signal for a dragon attack blares from a dozen trumpets. The whole camp springs into action. There's a huge commotion as sorcerers sprint to their appointed positions. Anumaris and Rinderan rush off to join them. Less than half a minute after the alarm, the sorcerous shield begins to glow faintly above us, just visible in the light of dawn. I take out my slate, ready once more to participate in the sorcerous relay.

'Good luck,' cries Droo, before swiftly rolling under the wagon. Overhead, dragons fly menacingly into view. Last time I was battered half to death. With any luck they'll kill me this time and I won't have to listen to Droo and Rinderan speculating about my personal affairs. There's a lot of noise, a lot of confusion, and a great deal of sorcery unleashed in a short space of time. Five minutes later, or perhaps more - it's difficult to be exact - I find myself lying on the ground, dazed, and not too sure how I got there. I ache all over. Droo is standing over me, prodding me awake.

'Captain Thraxas?'

I groan. 'What happened?'

'You were supporting the shield really well till you fell over when a big dragon came really close. Some sorcerers chased it off.'

Droo tries, and fails, to help me to my feet. I'm too heavy for her to move and I can't raise myself. 'Are you badly hurt?'

'Just bruised.'

'You did well again.' Droo is supportive. I appreciate it. I put a lot of effort into holding up that slate and there was no one else there to see it. Above us, the shield is still in place. The dragons have retreated, once more thwarted by our defensive sorcery. I still can't get up. I wonder if this hurts our sorcerers as much as it hurts me? Probably not. Lying on the ground, it strikes me that I should be investigating more Niojans. It's time I talked to Archbishop Gudurius, though I always find the religious fanaticism of Niojans off-putting. Their ordinary citizens can be bad enough. Their bishops are even more intolerable. I dread to think what their archbishops are like. However, Captain Istaros was a member of Ritari's special defence unit, and he's dead, and Ritari's main rival seems to be the Archbishop, so it's time I talked to him. Maybe I should have a word with Legate Denpir too. According to Hanama, the Legates are strong allies of the church.

I finally haul myself to my feet. 'Ensign Droo. It's time to investigate.' I sit down heavily beside the remains of the fire. 'Unfortunately I don't have the strength at the moment. I don't know how I'm meant to investigate anything when every few minutes I'm expected to hold off the Orcish dragon horde. 'Do we have any food?'

'I'll see what's left.'

A messenger rushes up. A young Elf, about Droo's age, with thick blond hair and an eager expression. Why Lisutaris's messengers are all so eager I don't know. They seem to enjoy rushing round carrying messages. 'Captain Thraxas, our commander requires your presence immediately.'

'I've just been struggling with dragons and I haven't eaten.'

'She said *immediately*.'

The Elf bounds off to torment someone else. I shake my head, and wearily haul myself to me feet again. 'Ensign Droo. I have an important mission for you.'

'Find some beer before you return?'

'Yes. Ignore all distractions. Kill anyone who gets in your way.'

I trudge towards our War Leader's command tent. I'm in a very bad mood. Lisutaris knows I'm participating in the defence against dragon attacks. She should know I'm currently battered, bruised, and hungry. Does she give me a moment to rest? No, she doesn't. The woman is a tyrant. I enter her command tent. Lisutaris is alone, save for Makri.

'Captain Thraxas. We need to talk.'

'Is it about the dragon shield? I've done my best but I really think I should be excused. I'm battered and–'

'You can't be excused,' says Lisutaris. 'We need your help.'

'But I–'

'You're not the only one who's been battered. There are other non-sorcerers in the relay who've suffered worse than you. I don't hear them complaining.'

'Probably because you're not listening. Really, it's ridiculous to assign me this extra duty. I'm already struggling with the incompetent bunch of misfits who've been assigned to my unit.'

Our Commander raises her eyebrows. 'Incompetent misfits? Rather a harsh judgement. Anumaris Thunderbolt reports you to be an excellent officer.'

'She does?' I'm surprised.

Lisutaris fixes her Commander's gaze on me. 'Yes. Until I ordered her to stop talking nonsense and tell me the truth. The truth does not reveal you to be an excellent officer, particularly in your treatment of Anumaris. If a young sorcerer is doing her best to obey orders and follow military procedures, I don't expect you to make her life miserable.'

'Well if you're going to bully the young woman into making up stories–'

'Enough, Captain Thraxas. I'm not an idiot. Your unit is quite satisfactory, particularly Anumaris. For some reason she's loyal to you. So treat her better, she's going to be a valuable asset for Turai. And start acting like a proper officer.'

'Yes, Commander. Was that all?'

'Far from it. I just received a message from Legate Denpir. He and Bishop-General Ritari are on their way to see me and they're not happy.'

'Niojans are never happy.'

'Now they're especially unhappy. King Lamachus has been sending them messages, demanding to know what happened to his nephew.'

'Why is he making such a fuss? King Lamachus isn't short of nephews. He's known for his large family.'

Lisutaris glares at me, not amused. 'Perhaps Istaros was a particular favourite. Now he's been murdered and the King wants to know why and he's putting pressure on his officers to find out. They're putting pressure on me, and isn't this exactly what I told you I didn't want to happen? Why haven't you solved it yet?'

'I've made some progress. My best guess is an internal Niojan power struggle.'

'*Guess*? Did you actually solve any crimes in Turai?'

'Number one chariot at investigating.'

'So you say. Yet now, on the one occasion I need you to produce results, you're floundering. Not good enough, Captain. I asked you to make sure this affair didn't bother me. Now it's bothering me.'

Captain Julius sticks his head through the tent flap. 'Bishop-General Ritari and Legate Denpir here to see you, Commander.'

'Tell them to wait.'

Lisutaris is still glaring at me. 'Well, Thraxas, you'd better do the one thing you're good at.'

'What's that?'

'Lying. Tell the General and the Legate something that makes it sound like you've been making progress. I don't care what. Just send them away with the notion that my security unit is actually doing something. I can't risk Bishop-General Ritari turning against me.'

Our War Leader summons the Niojans into her command tent. Legate Denpir is a smaller man than the last legate, Apiroi, but he doesn't look any friendlier. His sharp eyes dart around the tent as if suspicious of his surroundings and he wears the permanent frown of a Niojan official who doesn't trust foreigners. Bishop-General Ritari salutes Lisutaris formally. Denpir doesn't, which is a breech of protocol, though it may be because he's busy casting a loathing glance at Makri.

'Commander,' says the Bishop-General. 'King Lamachus has been in touch. His highness's envoy informs us that his majesty is not pleased.'

'I understand your concerns. We're doing all we can.'

'Captain Istaros was highly favoured by the King.' Legate Denpir has a deep voice, and speaks slowly, as if impressed by his own powers of oration. 'Last month he was promoted to the King's Special Advisory Council.'

'You've told me this before, Legate,' replies Lisutaris. 'And I've assured you we're doing everything we can to catch the murderer.'

'We deferred to your wishes that your own security staff investigate this killing. This has produced no results. King Lamachus is not pleased. His advisory council has suggested he may want to rethink his alliance.'

'No one is rethinking any alliances while we're almost at the gates of Turai.'

'King Lamachus does not answer to you.'

'His army does for as long as I'm War Leader.'

I can see this spiralling out of control. Perhaps Bishop-General Ritari does too, because he interjects in more reasonable tone. 'Has there been any progress with your investigation?'

'I believe so.' Lisutaris gives me a meaningful look. The meaning being that I'd better come up with something good.

'Well?' demands Legate Denpir. 'Have you made progress?'

'Great progress,' I reply, with confidence. 'I've a solid idea of what's been going on. I have more enquiries to make but I should have all the required evidence in a day or two.'

Legate Denpir is unimpressed. 'Can you tell us why Captain Istaros was murdered?'

'Not at the moment.'

He snorts in derision. 'Is that the best you can do?' He turns back to Lisutaris. 'I will not tolerate this contemptuous treatment of Nioj. If you continue to treat us unfairly-'

'Actually, I'm a well-known friend of Nioj,' I interrupt.

'What?'

'I've done a lot of work for Nioj in my time. Always helping out your citizens in Turai. King Lamachus once sent me a letter of appreciation.'

Legate Denpir almost explodes. 'This is preposterous!'

'Not at all. The first time I worked for Nioj involved the Niojan embassy in Turai. Tricky case where they were sure the Samsarinans had been spying on them. They were very complimentary when I sorted it out for them. Ambassador

Dimachus thanked me in person. After that the Niojans regarded me as a good man to have on their side. There was another awkward affair where the Niojan Ambassador's daughter was accused of stealing. Looked like a major international incident till I took matters in hand. I had to stand up to some important people in Turai to defend Niojan interests, but once I'm on a case, I don't back down. After I cleared the Ambassador's daughter's name, they were impressed enough to send a report to Nioj and the King's Legate wrote to me, thanking me for my efforts.'

'And so,' I say, in conclusion. 'You may trust that the investigation is proceeding smoothly, in the hands of a man who has, on numerous occasions, done excellent service for Nioj. I'll sort it this for you. Operational details need to remain secret for the meantime, but with your co-operation, I'll solve this mystery. You can depend on that.'

Denpir glowers at me. 'The King's Legate wrote to you?'

'Rather a fulsome letter. It's hanging on my wall in Turai.'

'So you see, gentlemen,' says Lisutaris. 'There could be no better man than Captain Thraxas to unravel this mystery. Now I really must bring this meeting to a close. Lord Kalith ar Yil is outside, waiting to see me on important business.'

Legate Denpir is nonplussed. He's not prepared to let things go, but Bishop-General Ritari, apparently satisfied that their affairs are safe in the hand of Thraxas, number one chariot at investigating, salutes our Commander and ushers the Legate out of the tent. Lisutaris turns to me. 'The King of Nioj wrote you a thank-you letter?'

Makri laughs, which is unprofessional of her. She stifles it quickly.

'No, I just made that up. I've never worked for Nioj.'

'You do have a talent for lying, I'll give you that.'

'What if Legate Denpir wants to see the glowing letter of thanks you have on your wall?' asks Makri. 'Given that it doesn't exist.'

'If we ever get that far we'll have chased the Orcs out of Turai by then. Who's going to care? Anyway, I could say it was lost during the war.'

'Have you actually made any progress with the investigation?' asks Lisutaris.

'Not much. But my lies will keep the Niojans happy till we reach Turai.'

'I suppose that's something. Do you think Archbishop Gudurius might be behind the murder?'

I'm surprised to hear this from Lisutaris. 'Why do you say that? Do you have some information?'

'Nothing that relates to this case. But I know Gudurius of old. I encountered him when he was a young Pontifex visiting Turai with his bishop. The bishop died not long after, and there was gossip among the Niojan sorcerers that Gudurius was responsible. He was promoted to bishop soon afterwards.'

'You're saying he's killed to advance his career?'

'So it was rumoured.'

It's an interesting piece of information, one I'll bear in mind when I interview the Archbishop.

'And now,' says Lisutaris. 'Kalith ar Yil really is waiting to see me. He's probably wondering where I was last night when he tried to contact me.'

'I take it you don't want him to learn you were indisposed in my wagon?'

'I'd rather he didn't.'

'I'll tell him something convincing.'

Lisutaris nods. 'I expect you will.'

'Maybe instead of making Thraxas your Chief of Security you should just have employed him to lie for you?' suggests Makri.

'Much the same thing, on occasion,' I reply. Bring in the Elvish Lord, I'll sort him out.

Chapter Thirteen

Not long afterwards I'm standing outside, halfway between the command centre and Makri's small tent, feeling pleased with myself. 'That went well,' I say to her. 'An Elvish lord is never going to be able to tell when I'm lying. Where he comes from everyone talks to the trees.'

'No they don't.'

'I remember a lot of talking to trees when we were on Avula. Anyway, tree-talking or not, Lisutaris is in the clear and I've once more rescued our War Leader from a tricky situation. And what about the way I bamboozled these Niojans? It's a gift, Makri.'

Makri claims not to be impressed. 'If you'd made more progress with your investigation you wouldn't have had to lie to the Niojans. If Lisutaris hadn't smoked too much thazis, you wouldn't have had to lie to the Elves. It's not really something to brag about.'

Makri's puritanical tendencies are re-surfacing, probably due to her irritation at being banished from the command tent. Lisutaris temporarily dispensed with her services as Tirini Snake Smiter was on her way. 'I don't trust Tirini to protect her.'

'The tent is surrounded by her personal guard. She'll be fine.'

'How do we know Deeziz the Unseen isn't creeping around?'

Deeziz the Unseen, the most powerful Orcish sorcerer, has baffled us in the past, infiltrating our ranks. 'Last time Deeziz appeared, Lisutaris came into direct contact with her. She says Deeziz can never come close again without her recognising her, no matter how she's disguised. I hope that's true. Anyway, don't you need time off? You're meant to be helping Arichdamis with his mathematics.'

Makri's shoulders droop. 'I know.'

'Then why aren't you hurrying in Arichdamis's direction?'

'You know why I'm not.'

'Still finding the mathematics too complicated?'

'Everyone would find it too complicated. Create a path through multiple dimensions so that protective sorcery may flow through a trench which zigzags through a space which is surrounded by hostile sorcery. Try not to kill anyone in the process. The whole thing is absurd. Yesterday Arichdamis told me he was sure he'd calculated the path through the fourth dimension properly but we couldn't check it any more because that might cause the figures to change and affect things when his sorcery reached the fifth dimension.'

I blink. 'What?'

'Some of the calculations can't be checked. We have to get the figures right, and go with that. If you check them again it changes things.'

'That doesn't make sense.'

'I know. None of it makes sense.'

'How can checking the figures change things?'

Makri shrugs. 'Arichdamis explained it but I got lost. Something about tiny packets of sorcery which exist in a place we can never precisely locate, and if we checked the figures again it would cause these tiny packets of sorcery to move somewhere else and ruin everything.'

'Is he insane?'

'I don't think so.'

'Drinking too much?'

'Not as far as I can see,' says Makri. 'He's always been abstemious.'

'But how can you check his figures if you can't check his figures?'

'I can check them before he writes them down in his final manuscript. But after that you can't analyse them any more. Not that I can really check them because it's too complicated anyway.'

Senior officers walk briskly by, on their way to the command tent for orders. We're not far from Turai and there's no rest for anyone.

'Makri, you're not making this plan sound very credible. Arichdamis might be a genius but I'm not sure about putting our fate in his hands. What about this other helper, Lezunda Blue Glow? Does he still understand all this?'

'He says he does.' Makri frowns. 'I'm not convinced. I don't get the impression he's such a great mathematical genius. I think he's in over his head, just like me, but doesn't want to admit it.'

Makri straightens up. 'I'd better get over there. I never thought I'd end up scared to attend a mathematics session. If I end up getting blamed for this disaster it's going to be really unfair. History will record that Makri the Orcish saboteur deliberately ruined things, thereby ensuring the final catastrophic defeat of the West.'

'You're worrying about that too much.'

'I'm not.'

Makri follows me to my wagon where Droo, Rinderan and Anumaris are standing around the campfire.

'Droo, have you located any beer?'

'No. Sorry. Everyone's extra careful since rations went low.'

'Rinderan?'

'Sorry, Captain. I have no leads on beer.'

'Dammit Rinderan, your family owns a brewery in the Southern Hills. I expected better of you.' I glare at them. 'As a security unit you're a severe disappointment.'

'We've been investigating things more important than beer,' says Anumaris, testily.

'I doubt it. What did you learn?'

'Three days ago a Niojan Captain committed suicide. Captain Taijenius. He was found dead in his tent having apparently taken poison.'

This is a startling piece of news. 'Suicide? A Niojan captain? Why didn't anyone hear about it?'

'They decided it was no one's business, and kept it quiet,' explains Anumaris.

'Did you learn why he did it?'

'No. The Niojan sorcerer I talked to didn't have many details. I asked if he knew of any connection between this Captain Taijenius and Captain Istaros but he couldn't tell me.'

I'm puzzled. 'Why would anyone make it this far in the campaign and then decide to do away with themselves when we're almost at Turai? I'll need to find out more. Good work, everyone.'

I dismiss my unit. They head towards to campfire to prepare food.

'They seem to be good at investigating,' says Makri.

'They're getting better. I've knocked them into shape. Time for me to get to work. Care to accompany me?'

Makri shakes her head. 'I should be with Arichdamis.'

'You can spare a few minutes. It won't take long.'

'No, I'd better get going.'

'Come with me. The change will do you good. Clear your mind.'

'Ha!' says Makri, quite incongruously. 'You want me to come along because you always investigate better when I'm involved.' She looks pleased with herself.

'Nonsense. I investigated fine before you arrived.'

'You're floundering. You always flounder when I'm not around.'

'That's the most foolish idea you've ever had, and you've had a lot of foolish ideas. Now come on, let's visit Major Stranachus.'

Makri follows along, looking smug. In truth, it has struck me that these days I am used to having Makri around during my investigations. Maybe I've been missing her during this one. Not that I'm about to admit anything of the sort to her.

'Really, you should have been paying me all along,' says Makri. 'Probably owe me about three year's wages.'

'Paying you? Without me looking after you, you'd have been thrown from the walls of Turai by an outraged citizenry. I just want you along because you'll annoy the Niojans.'

Even though the Niojans have become used to me, their perimeter guards still baulk at the sight of Makri. They question us about my business and show signs of refusing to let us proceed till I remind them of my rank. 'Head of our War Leader's personal security unit. Step aside or I'll have you arrested for interfering with the war effort.'

They let us through, glowering at Makri. We walk through their encampment. Everything is still tidy, all their troops smartly dressed, all in good order. How or why it is the Niojans maintain such discipline, I can't say. A product of their religious enthusiasm? Perhaps, though I've never noticed religious enthusiasm in Turai affect the behaviour of our corrupt bishops and pontifexes. Major Stranachus is sitting outside his tent, polishing his boots.

'Captain Thraxas? What can I do for you?'

'I want to know more about the suicide of Captain Taijenius.'

The major glances uncertainly at Makri, uneasy at her presence. 'I don't really know the details.'

'Was he a friend of Captain Istaros?'

'I've no idea. What does this have to do with–'

'Was there an investigation after he was found dead?'

'What sort of investigation would there be? He committed suicide. He left a note.'

'In Turai, we don't just believe any old note. Was there anything suspicious about the death?'

'Not as far as I know.'

'Were you involved in the investigation? Or non-investigation?'

'No, I wasn't. Captain Thraxas, I really don't see what that incident has to do with our present problems, the murder of Captain Istaros. Or the possible murder of Legate Apiroi.'

We stare at each other. Stranachus is trying to wrestle back control of the conversation by mentioning Legate Apiroi, knowing quite well that I also suspect Lisutaris and Hanama of being responsible for his death.

'I'd like to talk to someone who can tell me more about the suicide. Preferably not a Niojan officer with a well-prepared story.'

If not quite outraged, Major Stranachus is no longer polite. 'The suicide falls outside your remit, Captain Thraxas.'

'Nothing falls outside my remit. Point me in the direction of someone I can talk to.'

'Captain Taijenius had a younger brother,' says Stranachus, curtly. 'You'll find him with the fourth infantry on the west side of the camp.'

I walk through the Niojan camp with Makri. 'You finally managed to annoy Major Stranachus,' she says. 'And he was so polite before. Does this suicide have any real relevance?'

'Who knows? If Taijenius knew Captain Istaros, it might. Anyway, it's time we dug up some dirt on the Niojans, they've been digging up plenty on us. I'm still worried one of their sorcerers might disobey Lisutaris's orders and try looking back in time to the murder of Legate Apiroi.'

'Lisutaris is War Leader and Head of the Sorcerers Guild. Surely no sorcerer would risk disobeying her?'

'You can't trust the Niojans. They're almost as bad as the Simnians.'

We walk on through the camp.

'Is there any foreign population you don't object to? asks Makri. 'The Samsarinans perhaps?'

'Samsarinans are as bad as everyone else. You saw what they were like when we were there.'

'The Southern Hills?'

'Barely civilised.'

'The peoples of the furthest west?'

'Barbarians, all of them.'

'The far north?'

'Even worse barbarians. Gurd's the only decent man ever to come out of the north, and even he has problems. I tell you Makri, you got lucky when you ended up in Turai. The rest of the continent is full of ignorance and savagery. I'd let the Orcs conquer them all if it didn't mean Turai would suffer too.'

'You don't even like Turai. You're always complaining about it.'

'It's gone downhill in recent years. Here's the fourth infantry encampment. Time to find Taijenius's brother.'

Having located the Niojan Fourth Infantry, it doesn't take long to find Taijenius's brother. The first officer we encounter looks surprised to find a Turanian Captain in his ranks but he talks to me politely enough.

'The brother of Taijenius? You mean Arkius? Two rows down, third tent on the left.

Apparently Bishop-General Ritari's words have had an effect. The Niojans are finally co-operating. Or so it would seem till we meet Arkius, a surly young man, not quite as smartly turned out as his fellow Niojans. His tunic is unbuttoned, his boots are scuffed and he has the appearance of a man who's been drinking in private, enough for me to recognise the symptoms. He's sitting on a small folding chair in front of his tent and doesn't get up to greet us.

'We're here about your brother.'

'If Colonel Orisius sent you to convince me he committed suicide, forget it. I'm not listening to any more of his nonsense.'

I take seat beside him, uninvited. I pull out the slender silver flask I have hidden inside my tunic, the remains of my precious supply of klee. 'Tell me why your brother didn't commit suicide.'

He thinks about refusing the klee, decides against it, and takes a swig. 'He didn't kill himself. Taijenius would never have done that.'

'I believe you,' I say, and encourage him to take another drink. 'Tell me what happened.'

'Someone poisoned him. They faked his suicide.'

I'm dubious, though I don't let it show. It's not that easy to fake a suicide. 'He left a note. What did it say?'

'Some nonsense about being dishonoured because he couldn't pay a gambling debt. My brother never gambled in his life.'

'Was it his handwriting?'

Arkius glowers at me. 'It looked like it. But that doesn't prove anything. Someone could have forged it. Colonel Orisius accepted it as real because he wanted the affair to end as quickly as possible. It was humiliating to have one of his officers commit suicide. He didn't care about finding out the truth.'

'Did your brother ever express any sort of suicidal thoughts?'

'No!'

'Are you sure? '

Arkius leaps to his feat eyes blazing. 'My brother did not commit suicide! If you say it again I'll kill you!'

I remain seated. 'Tell me more about him. Did he know Captain Istaros?'

'They worked together. They were both in some special unit for Bishop-General Ritari. Protecting him from danger, he said.'

'Did he travel to Samsarina with Captain Istaros for the swordfighting tournament?'

'Yes. That's when they got in that fight.'

'Fight?'

'With the Archbishop's men.'

'You mean Archbishop Gudurius?'

'Yes. They were attacked by the Archbishop's guards. Istaros and my brother killed one of them. They had to leave Elath right after that.'

'Do you know why the Archbishop's men attacked them?'

'No, and I don't care. I'm tired of talking about this. My brother didn't commit suicide. Someone killed him.' With that, Arkius abruptly departs, disappearing quickly into the rows of Niojan tents.

Makri and I head out of the Niojan encampment. I glance at the sky, something I've been doing frequently since becoming involved in our dragon shield. It's clear and blue: a calm, peaceful day.

'Do you think his brother did commit suicide?' asks Makri.

'No. A gambling debt would be humiliating for a Niojan officer but not so bad he'd have to kill himself. Taijenius was probably murdered. Someone faked the suicide note. Not that hard for a competent sorcerer.'

'If two members of Ritari's defence unit have been murdered, it can't be coincidence.'

I agree. 'Captain Istaros and Captain Taijenius were both in Elath. They got in a fight with the Archbishop's men and killed one of them. Now they're both dead. The natural conclusion, I suppose, is that Archbishop Gudurius is taking revenge.' I halt and look around. 'Time to talk to the Archbishop. That large tent over there with the religious flag is where we'll find him, I imagine.'

The Archbishop's tent is larger than our War Leader's command centre; probably the largest tent I've seen on campaign. It's in better condition too, the Archbishop being a recent arrival.

'Why did he come here?' wonders Makri. 'I can't see an Archbishop storming the walls.'

'He won't be putting himself in danger. He's brought a troop of soldiers with him. Good for his status, I suppose.'

There are five or six soldiers between us and the Archbishop's tent, his insignia on their shoulders. We're still some way from the entrance when the first one hurries towards us, blocking our way. 'We're here to see–' I begin, but I don't get any further. The solider, quite a brawny warrior, draws his sword and yells at us to depart.

I'm used to not being a welcome visitor but from the way the soldier is glaring at Makri I'd say I'm not the main problem here. He's looking at her like she's some demon from Orcish Hell. Makri, never one to diffuse an awkward situation, immediately draws her own sword. Not her beautiful Elvish sword, but her Orcish blade, a vile black weapon from which the soldier steps back in alarm. The other guards hurry towards us, drawing their own swords so that in moments we're facing an armed mob of agitated soldiers. By this time my own sword is in my hand. I didn't really intend to draw it; it happened automatically when Makri drew hers. I can't let her face six foes unsupported.

'I'm Captain Thraxas. Head of security to our War Leader, here to talk to the Archbishop.' With all the swords waving around, it sounds faintly ridiculous.

'Get this Orc bitch out of here,' cries the soldier directly in front of us. Makri draws her second sword. Things are looking ugly. I really should diffuse the situation. I can't think how to do that. I don't seem to be thinking very clearly these days. The tent flap opens and the Archbishop appears, easily recognisable due to his fancy robe. Beside him is some junior cleric in a less fancy robe. The Archbishop strides forward. 'What is happening here?'

His troops surround him to protect him, though the Archbishop doesn't seem worried. He's tall, thin and white-haired, well over sixty but upright, with no sign of stooping with age.

'Put your swords away.' His men obey him, reluctantly. They look anxiously on as he walks toward us, more so because Makri still holds her sword in her hand. 'An Orcish weapon?' he says. 'You must be the woman with Orcish blood I've heard about.' He doesn't sound unfriendly. Makri isn't sure what to make of it, and remains silent.

'Captain Thraxas.' I announce myself. 'Head of Security. 'We're here to ask you some questions, Archbishop.'

The junior cleric, a few paces back, starts to protest. The Archbishop silences him. 'I thought this might happen. Very well Captain Thraxas. If you and your companion would like to sheathe your weapons, we can step into my tent and talk.'

By now I'm about as puzzled as Makri. The Niojan Archbishop, whom one might have expected to be utterly hostile, turns out to be unexpectedly civil. Perhaps it's a trick. We follow him into his large tent. I've abandoned all hope of any Niojan ever offering me any hospitality but the Archbishop confounds my expectations by taking a silver decanter from a shelf beneath a table and pouring out three goblets of wine.

'I'm sorry for the scene outside. My guards can be over-enthusiastic at times.' He hands me a goblet of wine and then offers one to Makri. 'How intriguing to meet someone who was actually born in the Orcish lands. You are–?'

'Makri. Ensign Makri.'

'There's been a lot of talk about you in the Niojan camp, Ensign Makri. They say you were a gladiator. Is that true?'

'I was. Then I slaughtered my Orc Lord and his entourage and escaped.'

'How fascinating! Can I see your weapon?'

Makri takes out he sword and the Archbishop actually touches it. I can hardly believe it. It should be the most taboo, untouchable item imaginable to a Niojan but Gudurius seems unconcerned by Niojan taboos. There's some writing on the blade, in Orcish characters. When he asks her if she can translate it, and she does so, telling him it reads "*Death to you, death to all*," in the common Orcish speech, he's delighted, and actually tells her he has a manuscript in Orcish that he's been looking to have translated for years, and perhaps she wouldn't mind having a look at it sometime.

So now Makri is getting on famously with the Niojan Archbishop. Soon they'll be discussing architecture. It's a surprising development but not one that's helping me with my investigation. I sip my wine, savour its unusually sweet taste for a moment, then interrupt their conversation.

'Archbishop, I came here to ask you questions about a murder.'

'Of course, Captain Thraxas. I apologise for delaying you. It's just so remarkable to meet someone from the Orcish Lands, particularly an educated woman like Ensign Makri.'

'What can you tell me about captain Istaros?'

'Very little. I was aware of his presence, naturally, as he was the King's nephew, but I've had no contact with him.'

'Really? Not even in Elath?'

The Archbishop seems less sure of himself. 'There was an incident in Elath. A member of my staff was killed. A very regrettable affair. At the time I wasn't aware that Captain Istaros was involved. That's something I only heard very recently.'

'You mean just before you decided to take revenge by having him killed?'

The Archbishop raises his eyebrows. 'I wasn't expecting that accusation to come quite so soon, Captain Thraxas. I thought you'd lead up to it.'

'I'm running out of patience. Especially with Niojans.'

Archbishop Gudurius smiles. 'Other nations do tend to find us trying. However, I can assure you, I had nothing to do with the death of Captain Istaros. Here–' he refills my goblet, and Makri's. Then he indicates the small wooden chairs that surround the folding table towards the rear of the tent. 'Please sit down. I'll answer any questions you have.'

Chapter Fourteen

We walk back towards our encampment.

'So what did you learn?' asks Makri.

'Niojan Archbishops have some very sweet wine. Too sweet, I'd say. Though he was generous with it, I'll give him that.'

'Anything else?'

'They deny everything. I'm suspicious.'

'You're suspicious because he was friendly. You never trust suspects when they're friendly.'

'It generally means they're up to something.'

Archbishop Gudurius denied any involvement in Captain Istaros's murder, or any other murder. 'Claimed not to know anything. Also claimed never to have been in Turai, though Lisutaris told us he was. Says he's never contemplated taking revenge for anything.'

'I liked him,' says Makri.

'You like anyone that calls you an educated woman.'

'You should try it sometime.'

'I can't believe he touched your sword. An Orcish blade. What sort of Niojan Archbishop does that? They're meant to be religious fanatics.' I come to a halt. I'm hungry and I want beer. I've been hungry and wanting beer for months and I'm sick of it. 'I can't solve this case. I've lost the ability.'

'What?'

'I don't know how to sort it out. I don't know who's responsible for anything. I've forgotten how to investigate.'

'That's ridiculous. Why would you forget?'

'I don't know. Not enough beer, maybe. Or maybe I'm just getting old. I wish Lisutaris had never made me her head of security. I'd rather be with Gurd in his platoon. Nothing to worry about except charging into Turai.' We walk out of the Niojan encampment, passing into the area occupied by the Simnians.

'It's not like you to just give up, Thraxas.'

'No. But it's not like you to give up either, yet here you are, avoiding your mathematics lesson. Perhaps no one can investigate or learn mathematics in the middle of a war.'

'Is this really such a complicated case?'

I shake my head. 'I can hardly tell any more. We're miles from the scene of the crime, there are dragons overhead, soldiers everywhere, and not a tavern in sight. It's not like tramping round Turai, finding things out. I always knew what I was doing there. Not like here.' I look up at the sky. I can't see any dragons, though Makri tells me there are several on the far horizon, circling, observing us.

'There are strands, details, loose ends. Normally I'd have a sense of how they fit together. Not here. Why was Istaros in Elath? Was he really buying property? How did he meet the Archbishop's guards? Why did they fight? Is the Archbishop really taking revenge for the death of his friend? Did he decide to kill Taijenius as well? If so, who faked his suicide? Then there's Magranos. A Samsarinan. His death doesn't seem to fit with the others.'

Next to a Simnian supply tent, Makri comes to a halt and turns towards me. 'Does it matter if you can't explain every detail? If it turns out the Niojan Archbishop was behind the killings, you'll still have solved the case.'

'Not really. I wouldn't have a culprit. I've no idea who the Archbishop might have recruited to do his dirty work.'

Makri shrugs. 'It doesn't sound like you'd ever be able to convict anyone anyway. The Niojans aren't going to let their Archbishop be accused of murder.'

'The Niojans are the ones who are pressurising Lisutaris to find the murderer.'

"They'll stop pressurising when you inform them it was probably their own Archbishop.'

'I suppose so.'

'Lisutaris will be happy as long as Ritari's in the clear.'

I almost laugh. 'Lisutaris thinks Ritari will be friendly towards Turai when this is over. I don't believe any Niojan will ever be friendly to Turai.' I look east. We're in familiar territory. 'We might reach Turai tomorrow. After that, who knows what anyone will care about?' I stare at the ground. The Simnian supply tent is unguarded. Outside are several sacks. I pull one open. Inside are some fresh-looking yams. I quickly bend down and tuck a few in my pocket.

'I never though I'd see you reduced to stealing yams.'

'I've gone lower.'

We walk on. I ask Makri how she's coping with her calculations. She shakes her head and sighs. 'Too badly to describe. Arichdamis gave me a page of figures to check and I just looked at them blankly for fifteen minutes then told him they were fine.' She shakes her head again. 'This sorcerous mathematics is a bad idea. We'd be better off just swarming up the walls with siege ladders.'

'We'd all be killed.'

'At least it wouldn't be my fault.'

'I have confidence in you.'

'I don't. I'm useless. Lezunda Blue Glow is useless. And I'm starting to doubt Arichdamis. What if he's just making it up as he goes along? Maybe these other sorcerers were right. We're all going to die. I'll never get to the university. Not that I deserve to go, seeing as I'm so stupid. Is there some sort of record for the most soldiers ever killed in one battle? I think we might be going to surpass it.'

'For God's sake Makri, cheer up. We're not beaten yet.'

'We soon will be,' she mutters, then falls silent, and remains gloomy all the way back to our tents.

Chapter Fifteen

I'm sitting in our wagon, trundling towards the city. We're close to our objective. In two hours we'll reach the Steepen Woods. When we're through that we'll be able to see Turai. For the first time there are skirmishes on the flanks as small groups of Orcs harass our outlying troops. Probably just a means of testing our strength but enough to make everyone aware that we'll soon be in battle.

'What'll happen when we reach the city?' asks Anumaris.

'Not much, most likely. We'll set up a defensive position and get ready to besiege the city.'

'Won't the Orcs attack?'

'I doubt it. If they felt strong enough they'd have tried to interrupt our advance before now. Prince Amrag's going to wait in the city and try to wear us down.'

Amrag might have more troops on the way from the east. That's one of the many variables we can't know for sure. Droo appears, running alongside the wagon before nimbly hopping aboard. She smiles, and brandishes a bottle of wine.

'Look what I got from Telith!'

Telith is another young Elf, attached to the Niojan contingent as an Elvish Liaison. I've been encouraging Droo to pump her for information, so far without success. I examine the bottle of wine. 'Comes from a decent Elvish vineyard. Good work, Ensign. Better open it and get it inside us before we reach Turai.'

Droo removes the wax stopper from the bottle with the well-practised ease of an Elf who's been drinking wine all her life. I'm about to raise the bottle to my lips when Anumaris interrupts.

'What about your investigation?' she demands.

Droo appears puzzled. 'What?'

'Captain Thraxas sent you to see what you could find out from the Niojan liaison. Did you learn anything? Or did you just concentrate your efforts on acquiring alcohol, as usual?'

I'm moved to defend Droo. 'No need to sound so harsh, Anumaris. I'm sure Droo did her best.'

'This is not satisfactory, Captain Thraxas. I should inform our commander that this unit spends more time drinking than investigating.'

'Inform the Commander? Run off and tell tales to Lisutaris, thereby getting your comrades into trouble? Have you no loyalty to your fellow soldiers? I ought to fling you off the wagon. Any more of your subordination and I will.'

Anumaris shows no inclination to back down. 'Lisutaris clearly instructed you not to drink, yet you do little else. Ensign Droo has hardly been sober since she got here. Not that I really blame her. How disciplined could she be with you setting such a bad example?'

I'm prevented from making an angry retort by Droo. 'I did learn something. Ensign Telith told me Major Stranachus has some evidence against Hanama.'

'What? Why didn't you say that earlier?'

'You seemed so happy about the wine, I didn't want to spoil it.'

'What evidence does he have?'

'They've found a Niojan soldier who saw Hanama in the Niojan lines when we went into battle. Close to where the Legate was found dead.'

'Did this so-called witness see Hanama attack him?'

'I don't think so. He just saw her in the vicinity.'

'That's bad enough.' Anumaris frowns. 'There was no reason for Hanama to be anywhere near the Niojan battle line. It's very suspicious.'

'It's only suspicious if it's true,' I point out. 'It's also very convenient. Stranachus could be making it up, trying to put pressure on us. Why would it only come to light now?'

'They weren't looking before. Legate Apiroi was presumed to have been killed in battle. No one was looking for a murderer until Major Stranachus became suspicious. '

I glare at Anumaris, not liking the way she's making sense. 'This case keeps getting worse.'

'Look,' says Droo, brightly. 'Here's Rinderan. Maybe he's discovered something we'll like better.'

The young sorcerer from the Southern Hills climbs into the wagon, his rainbow cloak, now dusty and frayed, trailing behind him. 'I've just found out that Makri was spotted close to the place Magranos was killed, about an hour before his body was found.'

'Who spotted her? Some lackey in the pay of Baron Vosanos?'

'No. A Samsarinan priest. Quite a reliable witness, I'd say.'

I shake my head. 'Excellent work, Rinderan. You've found a witness that puts Makri close to the murder of Magranos. And you–' I turn to Droo. 'You've found a witness that incriminates Hanama in the death of Legate Apiroi. We seem to be learning everything that's harmful to Turai.'

'I can't help it if I discover things we don't want to discover,' protests Droo.

'You could have tried less hard. How come you've all suddenly become so proficient at investigating, dammit? None of you were any good before.' I take a drink from the bottle of Elvish wine. 'Rinderan, was there anything else about Makri? Any suspicious behaviour?'

'No. Just that she was nearby.'

'Makri has been acting a little oddly,' says Anumaris.

'Has she?'

'I thought so, last time I encountered her. She didn't seem quite herself. I wasn't sure she even recognised me.'

Droo chimes in. 'I noticed Makri was acting weird too. I thought maybe she was jealous that Thraxas got together with Sareepa.'

I glare at the young Elf. 'Ensign Sendroo. Please never advance any theory again.'

'Why not? Maybe she was jealous. She's always hanging round with you. She followed you all the way to the Elvish Isles.'

I shake my head and grunt, unable to come up with a reply withering enough. 'If Makri's acting strangely it's because she's under pressure from her work with Arichdamis. The mathematics is very advanced.'

'I'm not good at mathematics,' declares Droo. 'Once on Avula I entered my poems in the junior competition for eight-line elegies. But it turned out I counted wrong. My poems only had seven lines.' She looks thoughtful. 'Of course, I had been drinking a lot of wine.'

'You can't count to eight?' Anumaris sounds incredulous.

'I can! Except I got it wrong that time, for some reason.'

'Did your poems have titles?' asks Rinderan.

'Yes.'

'Perhaps you miscalculated by including the title in the line count. I could see that happening if you'd been drinking.'

Droo's face lights up. 'That must have been what happened! Thanks Rinderan.'

'Could we get back to the subject in hand?' I say, loudly. 'Anumaris, look after things here. I need to talk to Lisutaris. If anyone comes here asking questions, deny all knowledge of anything. Understand?'

'I'm not very good at lying,' mutters Anumaris.

'Just follow my example.'

'I can feel my morals decaying.'

I pass her the wine. 'Drink some of this. You'll get used to it.'

Chapter Sixteen

The army is camped outside Turai. The bulk of our forces stretches in a semi-circle around the western half of the city. Further east, small units of mounted scouts are scouring the region, ready to warn us of any sign of Orcish reinforcements coming this way over the Wastelands. It's an unusual start to hostilities. Normally when battle commences I'd be charging towards the enemy in the middle of a phalanx of spear-carrying warriors. If those enemies happened to be behind enemy walls, I'd be charging towards them with a ladder in my hand. The siege of Turai starts with a collection of disparate, ill-matched figures standing in the midst of the strange light produced by the coming together of the sorcerous fields produced by the western sorcerers around us and the Orcish sorcerers inside the city. Turai is covered by a faint orange glow, the Orcish defensive shield. The land outside is covered by a faint blue glow, our own magic shield. Where these meet, the air turns a dull purple colour. So far there's been no attempt by either side to pierce the other's protection. Any such attempt would lead to stalemate if the calculations of Dearineth the Precise Measurer are to be believed.

Here, at the very edge of our protected territory, the digging is about to begin. Arichdamis is talking to the miners' overseer, Major Erisimus from the Simnian military engineering unit. He's an experienced engineer, so I'm told. He looks the part, rugged, weather-beaten, strong and broad; a man who's done a lot of practical work in the field. Not that I have that much confidence in any Simnian, experienced or not. Arichdamis is meticulously pointing out details in his plans. The zigzagging trench has to be dug exactly right, inch-perfect in each direction. Each angled turn needs to be precise. Beside them stand Lisutaris and her senior commanders, accompanied by a strong unit from the Sorcerers Auxiliary Regiment. Nearby are several other sorcerers whose task will be to send the sorcery down the trench. Lezunda Blue Glow stands behind Arichdamis, looking relaxed. Next to them is Makri, carrying a scroll and looking uneasy.

Coranius the Grinder is close to Lisutaris. I wonder if he remembers the Samsarinan High Priestess's oracle? *'Glorious ending,'* she told him. That didn't sound to me like the greatest prophesy a man could have. Depends when it comes, I suppose. Could be years away. Or it could be soon. The tall walls of Turai look ominous. I'm not convinced we're going to make it inside without heavy casualties. Dearineth the Precise Measurer may believe we've enough sorcerous power to hold off the Orcs off but we've underestimated their power before. Deeziz the Unseen has outsmarted us.

Some way away from the crowd, Tirini Snake Smiter looks bored. She's here adding her power to the defence of Lisutaris. While I've come to accept she actually is powerful, I've never seen her in full-scale battle. I can't imagine it. I don't even know if she's an official member of the Sorcerers Regiment. I've never seen her wear any sort of uniform or insignia, or show the slightest regard for military protocol. In contrast to Tirini, Sareepa Lightning Strikes the Mountain stands alert in the company of six sorcerers from Mattesh; her guild are part of the trench squadron. If we succeed in undermining the walls, they'll be among those leading our troops into the city.

I gaze over at Turai. The western wall is tall enough to hide most of the buildings beyond, with the exception of the palace, towards the northern edge. Several familiar towers are no longer there, destroyed when the city fell. How much additional destruction there's been is impossible to say. Are the gleaming, white marble Law Courts around Golden Crescent still there? What about Lisutaris's beautiful mansion in Truth is Beauty Lane, where all the best sorcerers live? I notice Gurd looking at the walls too, and I know what he's thinking. He's wondering if his beloved tavern, the Avenging Axe, still stands. If it does, it will be occupied by Orcs. I clap him on the shoulder.

'Don't worry Gurd, we'll get rid of them.'
'I hate to think what they might have done to my tavern.'
'Probably won't have caused any more destruction than I did.'
Gurd nods. 'True. You were always breaking something.'

An odd noise makes us look up. A clattering sound. Arrows launched from the walls of the city have struck our sorcerous barrier. The barrier deflects them easily enough.

'Catapult!' shouts an officer. We watch as a large stone ball hurls through the air towards us. Normally I'd be scrambling for cover and so would everybody else. Not wishing to show a lack of confidence in the power of Lisutaris and her fellow sorcerers, we all stand there watching as the huge lump of stone flies towards us. It gets disturbingly close before hitting our barrier and disintegrating. Lisutaris nods. 'Begin the dig.'

Major Erisimus motions to his men. They set to work, breaking the first clods of earth from the trench that will take us to the walls of Turai. As all eyes turn to the start of the operation, I manage to get close enough to Lisutaris to whisper in her ear. 'Some investigating I need to tell you about.' Lisutaris allows herself to be drawn back a little way from the crowd. I bring her up to date on the state of operations, still keeping my voice down. 'I think Captain Istaros was killed as part of a feud between Archbishop Gudurius and Bishop-General Ritari.'

'Who was behind it?'

'Probably the Archbishop.'

'Good,' mutters Lisutaris. 'If you get evidence he murdered the King's nephew I can threaten to blackmail him if he looks like causing us trouble.'

'I'll do my best. It's not all good news. The Niojan investigator says he's got a witness that Hanama was close to Legate Apiroi when he was killed, which is suspicious. And some Samsarinan priest claims he saw Makri close to Major Magranos just before he was murdered.'

'Do whatever is necessary to clear their names.'

'Like what? Murder the witnesses?'

'Would that be possible?'

'No! I wasn't serious. I've never murdered a witness. Bribed some, on occasion.' I halt. 'That might be possible. Do you still have all the gold we won in Samsarina?'

Lisutaris produces a small purse from inside her cloak, a magic pocket, capable of holding almost anything. 'Still in here, most of it. I had to spend some on hospitality for senior officers.'

'Hospitality for senior officers? I take it that came from your share?'

'I hadn't really considered it. But no doubt you, Captain Thraxas, would be keen to do your part in securing our military alliances?'

I hope our commander is joking. She might be. She becomes serious again. 'I must get back to the trench. Do what you can to keep all this quiet. I'm relying on you.'

Lisutaris leaves, walking briskly towards the trench where the earth is piling up as the diggers continue their work. Arichdamis is talking to Coranius the Grinder, giving him instructions for the first spells that have to be cast for protection. Sareepa and her fellow sorcerers listen on. Lezunda Blue Glow is beside them but Makri hangs back a few paces, eyeing proceedings with distaste.

'The more I see of this, the more I like the idea of charging the walls with ladders.'

'Still struggling with the mathematics?'

'Arichdamis could be bouncing the sorcery off all three moons for all I know.'

'Does it matter that the sorcerers who're casting the spells don't understand it?'

Makri doesn't think so. 'Arichdamis tells them where to point their sorcery and they follow his instructions.'

Piles of earth are being removed from the trench and loaded onto small trolleys to be wheeled away. Nearby on the ground is the portable wooden roof that will slide along on top of the trench, protecting the diggers.

'Do you need me to investigate anything?' asks Makri.

'That depends. I'm going to talk to the person who says he saw you close to where Magranos was murdered. Feel like joining in with that?'

Makri's hand edges towards her sword. 'He's lying. I'll kill him if he says it again.'

'Probably best you don't come with me. Maybe you can help me afterwards, when I talk to the person who saw Hanama close to the place Legate Apiroi was killed.'

'Are you making this up to annoy me?'

'No. Actual witnesses can implicate both you and Hanama in murder.'

'Wasn't that what you were meant to be preventing? I'm sure I head Lisutaris say that.'

'Mainly I was meant to be preventing scandal over the murder of Captain Istaros. Keeping the Niojans happy.'

'How's that going?'

'So far I haven't started a war. It might still come to that.' I draw a silver flask from my tunic and sip from my klee. Risky, with Lisutaris in the vicinity, but I don't feel like caring. Makri looks at me keenly. That probably means she's going to say something I don't want to hear.

'What's the matter Thraxas? You've got that same look you have when you lose at the race track. Have you been gambling?'

'I wish I'd been gambling. The war's closed all the stadiums.'

'Then what's wrong?'

I shake my head. 'I don't know. Something doesn't feel right. I'm meant to be clearing Hanama's name even though she's probably guilty...'

'You've done that before.'

It's true. I have. Once someone becomes my client I stick with them. I've got people off when they were guilty as hell.

'Is it because you don't like Hanama?'

'No, I don't much care about that. I've had plenty of clients I don't like. It's just...' I take another sip of klee. It's poor quality. Barely warms the throat. 'You remember, not long after you came to Turai, I had that case with Grosex? Apprentice to Drantaax the sculptor?'

Makri nods. 'I remember. I got a crossbow bolt in the chest.'

'Grosex came to me for help after he was accused of killing his boss. It was a confusing case, with the gold, and the warrior monks, and Sarin the Merciless. So confusing I might have been able to get him off.' I take another sip of klee. 'But I didn't. I let him be hanged.'

'He was guilty. He killed Drantaax.'

'I know. But he was my client. Sort of. I remember there was some confusion over whether he'd paid my retainer or not. The fact remains, I could have helped him go free instead of allowing the Guards to convict him. I feel bad about that.'

'Why? And why now?'

I shrug. I can't explain it properly. 'Just feels odd. Now here I am, trying to get Hanama off, when she killed Apiroi.'

'Hanama was only following orders.'

'I know. I intend to protect her if I can. I'm just wondering why I didn't do it for Grosex. I don't think I ever gave up on a client any other time. What was special about him? He deserved to hang? Plenty of people deserve to hang. Usually if they're my clients I protect them anyway.'

The conversation isn't making my gloom disappear. 'I don't know why I decided Grosex was different.'

'You were angry because I got shot by a crossbow.'

That's true. Makri very nearly died. She would have, without unexpected help from the dolphins in the harbour and their healing stone.

'I really don't think you've anything to feel bad about, Thraxas. All the time I've been in Turai you've helped people. Poor people who couldn't get help anywhere else. Plenty of them would have been hanged if you hadn't helped.'

'That doesn't help Grosex.'

'It was a confusing case. I'm sure Drantaax's wife was pleased when Grosex was executed. She'd say it was justice.'

'She and everyone else involved were all out for themselves. I don't even know what justice would have been.'

Makri takes a sip from my klee. 'You're right, this is poor. Hardly burns at all. Thraxas, I doubt you can be consistent all the time. I always thought Grosex deserved to hang. I still do. If you have doubts, well that will happen in a place like Turai. It's corrupt. Half of your cases involve people who've got themselves into trouble by acting badly. You do the best you can and sometimes it won't work. Sometimes you'll do things and then later you might think you got it wrong. You can't help that. No one can. Not even professors of ethics, and I've heard professors of ethics talk about it.'

'Do you ever have any doubts about killing people?'

'What sort of doubts?'

'That maybe they didn't deserve to be killed?'

Makri shakes her head. 'No. Not yet.'

There's a long pause, punctuated by the sound of digging.

'What are you going to do about the person who saw Hanama close to the Niojan lines?'

'First, find out if he's real. Stranachus might just be making it up to put pressure on us.'

'What about the person who says I killed Magranos? Is he real?'

'Yes, unfortunately. I'll talk to him. See if there are any obvious flaws in his story.'

'What if there aren't?'

'I'll bribe him or threaten him.'

'That's more like it, Thraxas.'

I let the subject drop. If it turns out Makri did kill Magranos, I'll do my best to clear her name but I'm not going to forgive her for it.

Half-way between Lisutaris's command tent and the encampment of the Sorcerer's Auxiliary Regiment, the dragon alarm sounds. I fumble in my pockets for my slate. Dragons are already pouring out of the sky. A large group are heading straight for Lisutaris's command centre. The sky erupts as they attack the sorcerous shield and the sorcerers below use their powers to reinforce it.

'I have to get back there,' says Makri.

'Why? How are you going to help?'

Makri doesn't reply because at that moment a dragon slams into the shielding above us and the shockwave sends us both tumbling.

'Shouldn't you be waving a slate?' cries Makri.

I clamber rapidly to my feet. Slate now firmly in hand, I hold it above me and yell at the dragon. 'Take that, beast!' Sorcery flows into the slate as the power of our own army's sorcerers takes effect. There's a downwards bulge in the magic shield above, but as I brandish the slate, it rises back into position. 'No dragon gets past Thraxas!' I yell, pleased at my success. Unfortunately, at that moment, another dragon swoops to join my foe. It's a strong, malevolent beast, with huge jaws and talons. Faced with two of the gigantic creatures, I start to wilt. Pain shoots through my wrist. I have a hard time staying upright. Both dragons batter at the sorcerous shield.

'Damn you!' I try to force the shield back upwards but I lack the strength. I crumple to the ground. The dragons continue their attack and the shielding above begins to buckle.

'Get up and wave the slate!' shouts Makri.

'There should be sorcerers helping me!'

Makri hauls me to my feet. She's much stronger than she looks. 'Hold the slate up!'

'I know what to do!' I hold up the slate with as much determination as I can muster. 'Stay back! No one gets past–' I get no further. Both dragons slam in to the shield simultaneously and I'm once more thrown to the ground, bruised and winded.

'Thraxas! Get up! The shield's going to break!'

It's no use. I can't move. I've taken too many blows. No one could stand up to it. I lie immobile on the ground.

'Give me the slate!' yells Makri.

'You can't use it. It takes specialist knowledge.'

'It's only waving a rock in the air.' Makri wrenches it from my hand. She stands upright and raises the slate high above her. For a moment or two, it looks like she's succeeded in driving the dragons back. Both hesitate. The sorcerous shielding rises and looks more secure. It doesn't last. Both dragons pound downwards again, snarling and breathing fire. They crash into the shield and the shock sends Makri crashing to the ground.

I stumble to my feet. 'I told you it wasn't so easy.' Prising the magic slate from Makri's fingers I once more raise it in the air. By now the dragons are only inches above my outstretched arm. The sorcerous shield is warping and twisting beneath the assault, distorting the dragons' shapes and making them even more terrifying. Outraged at everything, I draw my sword and brandish it right at their faces. 'I'll stab you with this!'

One of the dragons swipes the shield with its mighty tail and the blow sends me crashing back to the ground. 'You can't be doing it right!' yells Makri. She grabs the slate and stretches her arm up defiantly. 'No dragon can get the better of me!'

Another might swipe from a dragon's tail bends the sorcerous shield till it's only a few feet from the ground. Makri collapses in a heap.

'Very impressive, Makri. Good technique.' I take hold of the slate and desperately try to rise, though there's now very little room in which to do so. The sorcerous shield is giving way under the assault, forced down almost to ground level. Any second now it's going to shatter, letting the dragons through. Suddenly I feel the slate grow hot in my fingers, new power surging through it. Still lying on my back, I hold it in the air. Immediately the shield begins to rise. Moments later I feel a surge of sorcery streaking past as spells are fired into the shielding, sending it back to a safe height. The dragons spin away, defeated and frustrated. I lie on my back, arm still in the air, sore, battered, and almost unable to move. When I manage to turn my head, Sareepa, Coranius and Lisutaris are walking towards us. None of them seem flustered.

'What's been going on here?' demands Lisutaris. 'Why is Makri lying on the ground?' Lisutaris actually bends down and helps Makri to her feet. 'Ensign Makri, are you injured?'

'No, Commander,' says Makri, in a tone that suggests she doesn't want too much credit for her bravery. I struggle to my feet. No one helps me.

'Captain Thraxas!' says Lisutaris, sternly. 'Did you recruit Makri for the dragon shield? That will never do. Don't you realise how important she is to the war effort?'

I'm bridling with indignation. 'Important to the war effort? Do you realise I've been–'

Lisutaris isn't listening. She's too busy checking Makri's vital signs for any sign of damage. 'Doesn't seem to be concussed…no apparent injury. Makri, I appreciate your courageous actions, but we can't risk you in situations like this. Your mathematics are far too important. If Captain Thraxas finds himself in difficulties, let him deal with it.'

'Yes, Commander.'

'You should rest. Perhaps we should call a herbalist, you're looking shaken after your ordeal.'

I've had enough of this. 'Ensign Makri will be just fine, particularly as I half-killed myself keeping two dragons off us. I'm off to eat with Gurd and Tanrose. Makri could do with some food inside her scrawny frame. I'll see she gets there without injuring her delicate features.'

Lisutaris looks at me pointedly. 'See that you do, Captain Thraxas. Gurd and Tanrose are good citizens. I can trust *them* to look after Makri properly.' She puts plenty of emphasis on *them*. I salute briefly and walk off, reflecting quite bitterly that even if I'm used to it by now, it's scandalous the way my efforts on behalf of Turai have always been belittled by our leadership.

Makri catches me up. 'It was difficult holding that slate,' she admits.

'I'm glad someone acknowledges it. Did you notice the way Lisutaris didn't hesitate to criticise me in front of Coranius and Sareepa? The woman is incompetent. She has no idea how to inspire an army.' We walk the short distance to the space set aside for the assistants to the Sorcerers Auxiliary Regiment. Tanrose is busy at the campfire as I hoped she would be. We arrive just as Gurd is sitting down to eat.

'It's just one thing after another. First a dragon attack, now Thraxas is here. Everyone grab some food while you still have the chance.'

I ignore this, and address Tanrose politely. 'Tanrose, I've been working all day and these dammed army rations aren't enough to keep a strong man going.'

Tanrose ladles stew into a bowl, puts the bowl on a tray with yams and bread, and passes it over.

'You're an angel in human form and a far better woman than Gurd deserves. I'd never have lasted this long without you. First thing we have to do when we take back the city is make sure the kitchen at the Avenging Axe is back in good order.'

'Tanrose will probably have other things to do,' says Makri.

'Like what?'

'Put her life back together. You can't expect the entire reconstruction effort to be focused on your stomach.'

'I don't see why not. If it wasn't for me we'd never have got this far. Not that Lisutaris shows any appreciation. I tell you, the way I've protected that woman from harm, the city ought to be putting up a statue of me in the palace grounds.'

'A statue?' Makri laughs. 'There wouldn't be enough marble. Probably have to dig a new quarry.'

'I deserve it. Free dinners for life too, if they really wanted to show their gratitude.'

'That would bankrupt the city.'

'You might get the award for first into Turai,' says Gurd. 'We're going in by tunnel and you'll be near the front.' He turns to Tanrose. 'We've been at a few sieges together. First man inside the city usually gets an award. As an incentive, you know. But mainly that happens by climbing siege ladders. Not really Thraxas's strong point.'

I bridle at this. 'I've climbed plenty of siege ladders in my time.'

Noticing that I've nearly emptied my plate, Tanrose leans over and spoons more stew in my direction. 'Leave Thraxas alone,' she says, scolding Gurd and Makri. 'He's been away from home for too long. No wonder he's missing his proper meals.'

'Thank you Tanrose. You're a beacon of civilisation in the midst of northern barbarians and pointy-eared intruders from the east. Is there any more bread? I've had a very hard day.'

Chapter Seventeen

The Samsarinan priest isn't hard to find. Unlike the Niojans, the Samsarinans didn't bring too many of them. I'm swiftly directed to a tent set up at the edge of their allotted space, a tent a little larger than those used by the common soldiers though not outrageously so. Pontifex Agrius is a sturdy-looking man with a knife at his belt, which makes me think he's at least seen some sort of action. I've met this sort of priest before, travelling with the army, ready to get their hands dirty. My favourable impression doesn't last. On learning of the reason for my visit he's dismissive. 'You're here to question me about the Orc woman? I've no time for that.'

'I won't take long. Just tell me when you saw Makri.'

He answers will ill-grace. 'I already told Baron Vosanos. I don't see why I have to repeat it to you. But if I must, then I saw the Orc woman - if she truly counts as a woman, which I doubt - not fifty yards from Major Magranos's tent. As I explained to the Baron, this was close to the time of Magranos's death.'

'How close?'

'I can't say, exactly. When I walked back that way, less than an hour later, he'd been killed. I rushed to help but other than praying over his remains, there was nothing I could do.'

There's nothing particularly convincing about his story. There's nothing particularly unconvincing either. I've been asking people questions for a long time and have a good sense of when they're telling the truth but it doesn't work with everyone. Priests can be difficult to read; they've often learned how to be persuasive.

'Do you have any other evidence that Makri was involved? Apart from seeing her near the tent?'

'None whatsoever. I'm not claiming she was involved. I merely report what I saw.'

Or else he's reporting what Baron Vosanos wants him to say he saw. It's still a troubling piece of evidence against Makri. Not enough to condemn her, but it looks bad if she was wandering around at the scene of the crime right before Major Magranos was killed.

'Why were you there?'

Momentarily, the Pontifex looks vague. 'I'm not sure what you mean?'

'It's a simple enough question. Why were you close to Major Magranos's tent?'

He gathers his thoughts. 'Walking. Every evening I stroll around the Samsarinan encampment, thinking of my sermon for the next day, and ministering to any soldiers who feel the need of spiritual assistance.'

'You must be a great help to them.'

'I do my best.'

'Do you always take the same route? Or did you just happen to walk that way that evening?'

He scowls at me. 'Are you implying I'm being less than honest?'

'I might be,' I say, deciding I've been polite enough so far, and wondering what a little hostility might produce. It produces no results. He looks vague again, and stares into the distance.

His is eyes focus on me again. 'You were saying?'

I learn nothing more from Agrius. He took his normal night-time stroll and happened to see Makri close to Magranos's tent, close to the time he was murdered. I thank him then depart. He wasn't the worst priest I've ever encountered. There again, he didn't offer me any refreshment, which is a breach of hospitality. You might expect more from a religious man. Overall, he seemed to find it difficult to concentrate on my questions. I'm not sure why.

I walk back through the Samsarinan encampment. The general atmosphere isn't bad. Quieter than it was on our long march, but still positive enough. I can see a lot of young soldiers talking good-humouredly to their companions. Apparently everyone still trusts Lisutaris and her plans. There's no hint of dissent, even in these unnatural circumstances, with a magical shield above us and a sorcerously protected trench zigzagging its way towards our enemy. Lisutaris has brought the army here in good order, protected them well, fed everyone sufficiently, and scored a notable victory over the Orcs. It's hard for anyone to argue with her abilities as War Leader. I'm almost optimistic till it strikes me that no matter what happens, a lot of these young soldiers will die when we enter the city. If we fail to enter the city, a lot more will die. I must be getting old. I never used to let things like that worry me. I should ask Gurd about it. He used to charge into battle in high spirits, caring for nothing. I wonder how he feels now? He's older too, with Tanrose to live for.

When I reach my security unit I talk to Rinderan. 'I'm suspicious about the Samsarinan priest. Disguise yourself and follow him without being observed.'

'How should I disguise myself?'

'A kitchen worker. Or porter. Something like that. Use you initiative.'

'Yes, Captain.' Rinderan looks doubtful. 'Won't I be conspicuous if I'm following him?'

'The point is not to be. Again, use your initiative. Follow him, don't get caught, and let me know if he does anything unusual.'

'Yes Captain.' Rinderan salutes, still doubtful, but eager enough to carry out his assignment. I'm out of ideas so I do nothing else for the rest of the day. Late in the evening Sareepa arrives, carrying beer, and we retire to the wagon where we spend the night.

Chapter Eighteen

I'm shaken awake. It takes me longer than usual to come to my senses. When I finally manage to open my eyes Makri is kneeling over me.

'Thraxas,' she hisses.

'Have the Orcs attacked?'

'No–'

'Then leave me alone.'

I close my eyes. Makri shakes me again. 'Wake up! It's important.'

I'm still groggy. 'What time is it?'

'Six in the morning.'

'Go away.'

'Arichdamis is dead!'

This gets my attention. 'What? When?'

'Half an hour ago.'

'Meet me outside.'

Makri nods, and withdraws. I rise without waking Sareepa, dress quickly, then slip out through the canvas. 'Tell me what happened.'

'I heard voices so I went outside. Arichdamis was lying on the ground with a sorcerer and a healer trying to help him, but they couldn't. He was dead. He had a heart attack.'

I'm now fully awake. 'A heart attack? For real? Or sorcery?'

'Coranius was there. He thought it was real.' Makri suddenly looks overwhelmingly sad. She was fond of the elderly mathematician, and she respected him. 'Coranius sent for Lisutaris,' she tells me. 'They're having a meeting now. But I haven't told you the worst part.'

'There's something worse than Arichdamis dying?'

'Yes. I was wondering what to do, when Lezunda Blue Glow appeared. I told him Arichdamis was dead and now he'd have to take over the calculations. He went pale. Or I think he did, it was hard to tell in the moonlight. He didn't look happy anyway. Then he admitted he didn't understand any of Arichdamis's mathematics and he'd just been pretending all along. I knew it! Didn't I tell you was a fraud! Standing there nodding and taking notes while Arichdamis was explaining things. What an imposter!'

'What did you say to him?'

'I didn't get the chance to speak. Right after admitting he didn't understand anything, he got on a horse and rode out of camp.'

'You can't be serious.'

'I am! He's fled!'

I shake my head. This is a lot to take in. Makri asks if I have any thazis. I hand her my small bag and she takes one of the sticks I've rolled, inhaling from it deeply. 'Will you come with me to talk to Lisutaris?' she says. 'I can't face her on my own.'

'Why not? What's wrong?'

'What's wrong? We're digging a trench that depends on Arichdamis's mathematics for protection. Except Arichdamis is dead and the other person who can do these calculations can't really do them and he's run away. That only leaves me.' Makri looks anguished. 'And I can't do them either. How am I going to explain that to Lisutaris?'

Makri's anguish increases. 'This is exactly what I feared. The attack plan is going to fail and our army's going to get slaughtered and everyone will blame me.'

'Only those who weren't slaughtered.'

'Don't make jokes about it! What am I going to tell Lisutaris?'

'The truth. As quickly as possible.'

Makri hangs back. 'I don't want to go.'

'You've no choice. Lisutaris has to know.'

Makri follows me, unwillingly. She turns and looks into the dark void to the west. 'Could I flee on a horse too? Would that be a bad thing to do?'

'In the present circumstance, very bad. Let's go.'

Makri comes to a halt. 'I can't do it. Some things are just beyond me. Like talking to that Elf I was involved with. I couldn't talk to him sensibly. And now it turns out I can't talk to our War Leader and admit I can't do the mathematics.'

'You told me you were getting the hang of it.'

'I was getting the hang Arichdamis's first four dimensions. Five and six are still a mystery.'

I take Makri's hand. 'Let's go.'

She looks downwards. 'Are you holding my hand?'

'Yes.'

'I'm not a schoolgirl. I can walk unaided, you know.'

I let go of Makri's hand and walk on. She comes to a halt and looks hopeless. 'I can't move.'

I take Makri's hand again and we walk towards the command tent to find Lisutaris. In the early morning light there's activity around the command centre though not as much as I'd expected. A few messengers can be seen, and some mid-level officers conferring among themselves, but there's no sign of panic. Arichdamis's death is a serious blow but no one realises how serious. By now Makri is managing to walk unaided but her place slows as we approach. Coranius the Grinder emerges from the command tent and walks off without acknowledging us.

'Looks like Lisutaris is on her own. Come on.'

Makri hesitates. 'Could it wait?'

'No.'

Makri remains rooted to the spot. I grab her hand again and we advance towards Lisutaris's command centre. As we pass the guards outside, Lisutaris herself appears in the doorway.

'Captain Thraxas. Ensign Makri. Are you holding hands?'

'No Commander!' says Makri, rapidly withdrawing her hand from mine. Lisutaris gives us a quizzical look but doesn't comment.

'We need to talk to you urgently, Commander. Or rather Makri does.' We follow our War Leader back into her tent. It smells of thazis but is in good order.

'I don't have much time,' says Lisutaris. 'With Arichdamis's unfortunate death I'll have to talk to our engineers about rescheduling. Hopefully with Lezunda Blue Glow in attendance it won't have any major impact.'

'About that...' says Makri. She falls silent.

'Yes?'

Makri screws up her features. 'Lezunda Blue Glow can't do the mathematics. He was only pretending he could. He told me that right before fleeing the encampment on horseback.'

Lisutaris is startled by the news. 'This can't be true.'

'It is. The calculations are too complicated. He couldn't cope.'

Our Commander looks shaken. She takes a thazis stick from inside her robe and lights it by snapping her fingers. 'Has he really fled?'

'Yes. And what's more-'

Lisutaris holds up her hand. She strides to the entrance and slips through the tent flap where she summons one of her young messengers. I hear her issuing instructions. 'Lezunda Blue Glow has fled the encampment. Inform Coranius the Grinder. Tell him to take Captain Lanius and four cavalrymen and bring him back immediately.'

'Yes, Commander.'

Lisutaris re-enters the tent. 'Damn that Lezunda. How dare he pretend to understand sorcerous mathematics? I'll make him regret it. Well Makri, it's up to you. I didn't want to saddle you with such responsibility but from now on we'll be depending on your skills.'

'You can't!' wails Makri. 'I don't understand it either.'

Lisutaris goes rigid. A small trace of sorcerous purple appears in her eyes, not something I've seen before unless she's casting a major spell. 'What exactly don't you understand?'

'Arichdamis's calculations. I understand some of it. But then it just becomes too complex.'

Lisutaris regains the power of movement and takes a step towards Makri. There's a definite purple tint to her eyes. 'Are you telling me, Ensign Makri, that my plan of attack, the plan I've persuaded my army to follow, the plan that depended on Arichdamis's calculations, and which in consequence I carefully safeguarded by appointing not one but two back-up mathematicians, cannot now proceed because both back-up mathematicians were lying about their skills?'

Makri starts to hang her head, but changes her mind, stands up straight and looks Lisutaris in the eye. 'Yes, Commander. That's what's happened. I apologise for my part in it.'

'You *apologise*?' Purple sparks begin to dance around Lisutaris's fingers. 'You *apologise*? What good is that?' She takes a step towards Makri. I hurriedly get between them, not wanting to see Makri struck down on the spot.

'Lets talk about this more. It may not be a total disaster.'

'And how not?' growls Lisutaris, directing her purple-tinged eyes towards me, which is an uncomfortable experience.

'Arichdamis's calculations have worked so far. The trench is heading towards the walls and the Orcs haven't been able to touch it. All the generals who thought you were crazy are now saying it's a brilliant plan.'

'What do you mean, *my generals thought I was crazy*? Never mind that. What good is this if we can't carry on?'

'Makri's learned all the mathematics up to this point. It just takes her a while to fully comprehend it. No disgrace in that. It involves previously unknown dimensions, whatever that means.' I turn to Makri. 'I think you can do it. Just take things more slowly. I'm sure you can work out the calculations necessary to get us to the walls.'

The intimidating purple glaze fades from Lisutaris's eyes, without vanishing completely. 'Makri, is that true?'

'I don't think so.'

'I think it is,' I say. 'You couldn't follow it at all at first but now you've mastered a good part of it. The problem is you're worrying too much. No surprise, really, when you're surrounded by people who don't have faith in you. It's not as if everyone is as supportive as I've always been.' I turn to Lisutaris. 'What are the alternatives? What would happen if you called off this plan?'

Lisutaris shakes her head. 'Nothing good. We'd be right back where we started. Worse, in fact. Hanama's intelligence unit reports that an Orcish relief force is already making their way across the wastelands. If we don't get into Turai in the next few days we'll have to pull back or suffer heavy casualties. Not that it would be my decision. The Niojans and Simnians won't support me after this fiasco. They'll elect a new War Leader.' Lisutaris lights a thazis stick. 'Makri, is what Thraxas says true? Could you do it?'

Makri shakes her head. 'I don't think I could.'

'What about Lezunda Blow Glow? Is he completely useless? If you took over, could he help?'

'No. He really is useless.'

'What about someone else?' I suggest. 'There must be one person among all these soldiers and Elves and sorcerers who has mathematical skills. If you had decent support, you could carry on while they helped check the figures. We'd only have a delay of a day or so.'

'I suppose so.' Makri doesn't sound convinced.

The pungent aroma of Lisutaris's thazis fills the tent. 'There would be the problem of convincing my senior officers to trust themselves to calculations carried out by Makri, her being a female with Orcish blood.'

'You're right,' cries Makri. 'They'll never agree to it. Best think of another plan.'

'Perhaps we could work around it,' says Lisutaris, crushing Makri's hopes. 'When Coranius brings Lezunda back into camp, we'll pretend he's now in charge of all mathematics. He can keep up public appearances. Meanwhile Makri will perform the calculations, aided by the excellent mathematician that Thraxas is now going to locate.'

'Will Lezunda agree to that?'

'He will if he doesn't want me to explode his head. Captain Thraxas, find a mathematician. Ensign Makri, start studying the relevant equations.'

Chapter Nineteen

Some hours later I arrive back from the Elvish section of the encampment feeling moderately satisfied. Accompanying me is an Elvish architect who, I am assured, is the most talented mathematician to be found on the island of Avula. So Lord Kalithar-Yil insisted anyway. I've encountered Lord Kalith before and while he doesn't owe me any favours, he did respond to Lisutaris's appeal for help favourably, not finding it strange that assistance might be required after the demise of Arichdamis. I make it clear that we're not in any serious trouble as the redoubtable Lezunda Blue Glow is well in control of the required calculations. Nonetheless, it would be helpful to have some assistance in checking his figures. Lord Kalith sent for the architect in question, an Elf by the name of Sorelin. He looks young to be an architect, but I'm not really certain what Elvish architects do. I've been on Avula and the dwellings were mainly wooden constructions in trees. Perhaps that takes a lot of planning, who knows? Anyway, not long afterwards I'm taking him to Lisutaris's command tent.

'I'm not familiar with Arichdamis's most recent work.'

'Just a matter of inventing new dimensions, so I'm told.'

Sorelin, who's tall, blond and good-looking in a way I've come to find annoying, isn't confident. 'New dimensions? I'm not certain what that means.'

'You'll get the hang of it. First we have to call in and see our War Leader.' I stride past the guards like the important figure in the war effort I've become, ushering the Elf inside the command tent. 'Commander, this is Sorelin, architect and mathematician. Best available on short notice.'

Lisutaris crosses over to face Sorelin. He salutes, and begins to speak but she ignores his words, instead gesturing with her hand so that a faint purple light envelops him. The young Elf looks startled. 'What's this?'

'A spell of secrecy. What I'm about to tell you is highly confidential and must not be repeated, even to your Elvish Lord. If you do repeat it, the spell will kill you, quite painfully. Are you clear about that?'

'Yes,' says Sorelin, alarmed.

'Good. The fact is, we're in trouble. Our chief mathematician has died and his subordinate is not up to the task. We do have a replacement, Ensign Makri, my bodyguard.'

'Ensign Makri? You mean the Orc woman?'

'Yes. But don't call her that.'

'Is she a mathematician?'

'Yes,' says Lisutaris. 'And stop asking questions. You're to assist Makri in every way possible. Read Arichdamis's writings, familiarise yourself with his works, and help Makri in her further calculations. Don't tell anyone what you're doing. Is that clear?'

'Yes, Commander.'

I escort Sorelin from the tent towards the trench. He's silent till he sees Makri at the head of the trench, studying a scroll. 'I don't want to help the Orc woman calculate!'

'Don't call her an Orc to her face. If you do she'll probably kill you faster that Lisutaris's spell.' We draw close. 'Ensign Makri. I've brought help. Finest young mathematician in the Elvish lands.'

'No, I'm not,' protests Sorelin.

Makri looks at me with some annoyance. 'Well is he of isn't he?'

'Lord Kalith-ar-Yil said he was. Builds the best tree houses on the island. And now, having once more rendered you invaluable assistance, I'm off to hunt for beer. '

'Don't you want to see what I've been doing?'

'I'm really in need of beer–'

'Come with me!' There's an odd expression on Makri's face, as if she's over-excited. She grabs me and proceeds to drag me down the wooden steps that lead into the trench. It's eight or nine feet deep, the walls reaching over our heads. I follow Makri along the first stretch which points left till we reach the first turning as it zigzags to the right. As intended, inside the trench we're hidden from the city walls. Turai is no longer in sight. With no direct line of fire, the miners are safe from projectiles from the distant walls. Not so distant now, as we proceed along. Makri points upwards.

'You see that faint purple glow, inside the blue glow? That's our extra shielding. That's what we've been doing. Extra protection inside the general sorcerous shield.'

We're obliged to press ourselves against the wall of the trench as a load of earth is removed from the dig, two miners pushing a small wooden cart past us. As the pass, they greet Makri quite familiarly, having now become used to her presence. Makri leads me further along.

'Why are we here?' I enquire. 'I've seen a trench before.'

'Not as good as this one. Look how the extra sorcery turns this corner. It's brilliant. Arichdamis was such a genius. I knew his extra dimensions were a good idea.' Once again, Makri seems over-excited about a trench. Still, I reflect, she always has appreciated fine engineering. She's the only person I've ever heard enthuse about Turai's sewerage system. By now we're close to the front of the trench and can hear the sound of digging as the miners inch their way towards the city walls. Near the front the movable wooden roof has been dragged over their heads, giving additional protection to the workers as they advance. When we turn the final corner we come across four diggers, stripped to the waist, excavating the earth with picks and shovels. Two more stand behind them, loading the earth into a cart, while behind them stands the Simnian engineer, Major Erisimus.

'Ensign Makri!' Erisimus greets her cordially.

The trench is regular, well-constructed, with wooden slats on the walls providing extra support. All around us is the blue glow of the sorcery as calculated by Arichdamis and produced by Coranius the Grinder and Sareepa Lighting Strikes the Mountain.

'How long till you reach the walls?'

'Two days, barring interruption.'

I'm interested to see all this, but still in need of beer. Makri isn't letting me go yet. 'You see that purple light right at the end? That's the new bit of sorcerous protection. I calculated that.'

I'm puzzled. We're surrounded by miners who were not meant to know that Makri's now in charge of our mathematics. 'Wasn't that meant to be a secret?'

Major Erisimus shakes his head. 'A secret that Lezunda is a fraud? We've always known that. If he was really in charge I'd have taken us out of the trench. Ensign Makri can get the job done.'

'You trust her?'

'We do.'

Makri looks smug. I congratulate her on her achievement, though I'm puzzled by this abrupt turnaround. Only a few hours ago she was wreathed in gloom about her inability to cope, and now she seems full of self-confidence.

'I think I've been underestimating my mathematical prowess.' She turns to Major Erisimus. 'Understandable, with people constantly telling me I was useless. I'm not specifically blaming Captain Thraxas though he did once say I was a stupid Orc who couldn't count to three.'

I'm outraged at this slur. 'What? I'm the one who encouraged you. You wouldn't be here if–' My words are cut off by a blaring of trumpets, sounding the alarm.

'Dragon attack!' yell the miners, casting down their tools. They immediately flee along the trench, led back to the safety of our front lines by Major Erisimus.

I curse, quite vehemently. 'More dragons. We'd better get going.'

'Why?' demands Makri. 'We're safe here. We're protected by sorcery. I made the calculations.'

I take a few steps backwards to peer over the moveable roof. High above, descending rapidly, a dragon is heading straight towards us. I grab hold of Makri's arm. 'We have to go.'

Makri angrily frees herself. 'I'm not running away. I helped make the protection for this trench and I'm staying right here.'

'Are you insane? Do you see the size of that dragon? We don't know if the sorcery is going to keep it out.'

'Why not? Because I did the calculating? You don't trust me, do you? You're always like this. *Expect Makri to get everything wrong.*'

I glare at my companion. There's an odd expression in her eyes that I can't interpret and don't have time to think about. 'It's got nothing to do with trusting you! I wouldn't have trusted Arichdamis either! We've got to get back behind the main magic shield before it's too late!'

'Fine. Run away. I'm staying here, with people who trust me.'

'No one trusts you! The miners all ran away!'

'I have been continually persecuted by humans.' Makri folds her arms. 'I'm staying.'

I glance upwards. The dragon is around fifty feet away and it's opening its jaws. Flames are emerging and it shows no sign of slowing down. I've no idea how much a huge dragon weights but whatever it might be, it's about to slam into this trench and I don't want to be here when it happens. I don't trust the thin layer of sorcery to protect me, no matter how well it was calculated.

'Go on, run away,' says Makri. 'I know you've always despised me.'

'Dammit Makri, if this dragon kills us I'm going to punch you right in the face!'

There's no time for anything else. Flames are already spreading over the top of the trench. The sorcerous shield repels them but the next instant the enormous dragon slams straight into it, causing a miniature earthquake which throws Makri and me to the ground. The walls shake and earth pours over our heads. A wooden slat hits me in the face. I curse, then try to draw my sword, meanwhile looking upwards in horror at the sight of a gigantic dragon leaping up and down mere inches away, kept out by a layer of sorcery which is now seeming less and less suitable for the task. The beast is bellowing with fury and still breathing fire. Makri attempts to stand up then thinks better of it as a plank of wood whacks her on the shoulder. She slumps back to the ground. More earth begins to fall, shaken loose from the walls. I start crawling away but by now there's so much dust in the air I can't see where I'm going. I abandon the effort and sink to the ground.

'This is your fault!' I shout. Above ground there are more flashes of light, followed by renewed roars from the dragon. One of its monstrous feet is now right above my head. I'm appalled at the size of its talons. The beast loses its grip in the face of the purple light which, I realise, is sorcery coming from our own forces. Lisutaris and her companions must be attempting to drive it off. I lie there, choking on dust, outraged at my suffering which I blame entirely on Makri, and watch as the purple light slowly forces the dragon away. It's pushed into the air where it hovers, a few feet from the ground, before disappearing from view in a blast of black and purple, victim to one of the extremely powerful spells Lisutaris keeps in her repertoire for emergencies.

For a few moments we lie there in an eerie silence.

'I hate you,' I tell Makri. I haul myself to my feet, I'm covered with dust and badly shaken.

Makri gets to her feet, more agilely than I did. She glares at me. 'I can't believe you threatened to punch me in the face! How dare you say that to me, you fat oaf!'

'I'll punch you in the face right now! What's the idea of staying here like fools when we could have run to safety?'

'There was no need to run. I told you we were safe.'

'You didn't know we were safe! The sensible thing to do was run away. You just wanted to stay here so you could brag about your calculations working. What if they hadn't?'

'Well they did, didn't they?'

'You got lucky. Just guessed the answer, I wouldn't be surprised.'

'How dare you insult me like that!' Makri steps forward. Again, there's an odd expression in her eyes. It strikes me, as it should have before, that Makri is not entirely sober. She's not drunk, but she's been taking something. I don't get time to consider it because with no warning she suddenly strikes me in the face. I yell in annoyance and swing a fist at her. Too fast for me, she dodges out the way but there's not a lot of room in this trench and when I take another swing she finds herself backed up against the wall. Intending to knock her head off, I step forward again, Makri's sword flashes into her hand.

'So it's like that, is it? Fine!' I take out my own sword and prepare to fight. At that moment I'm unexpectedly paralysed by an unknown force, as is Makri, who stands like a statue, her sword in her hand and an ugly expression on her face. Footsteps sound behind me though I can't turn my head to see who's coming.

'What is going on here?' I recognise Lisutaris's voice. I hear her snap her fingers, cancelling her spell. Able to move again, I sheath my sword and turn round to find our commander looking both puzzled and angry.

'I come to check on your welfare and find you engaged in swordplay? Explain yourselves.'

Makri sheathes her sword, not pleased to have been caught brawling in an undisciplined manner. 'Sorry, Commander.'

Lisutaris walks to the end of the trench. She gazes at the thin sorcerous shielding, dimly visible in the daylight. She reaches out her hand, as if feeling it, then transfers her gaze to the shielding above us. She nods, apparently satisfied. 'Strong enough. That was a large dragon. The fact that we held it off bodes well for our enterprise. Congratulations, Ensign Makri.'

'Thank you, Commander.'

'I'd still like to know why you and Thraxas were brawling.'

Lisutaris has a bad habit of harping on about things which would be better left alone. 'It was nothing, Commander,' I say. 'Just a minor disagreement in the heat of battle.'

'Thraxas threatened to punch me in the face,' chimes in Makri, who does on occasion have something of the angry schoolgirl about her.

'What? Is this true?'

I glare at Makri. 'You just had to repeat that, didn't you?'

We start to walk back along the trench. It's still in decent shape though several of the supporting wall slats have come down and will need replacing. Behind me Makri is still complaining to Lisutaris. 'Thraxas has been wanting to punch me ever since I arrived in Turai. Just waiting for an excuse. His behaviour towards women is horrifying, there's no other word for it.'

'I know,' agrees Lisutaris. 'But you wont have to put up with it for much longer. Another two days should see us at the walls.'

I trudge on, refusing to engage. I'm battered, filthy and badly in need of beer. Failing that, some Elvish wine and some peace and quiet. When I approach my wagon and I'm intercepted by Hanama, I know I'm not about to get either.

Chapter Twenty

'Captain Thraxas, I have information.' Hanama lowers her voice. 'My unit intercepted messages sent by Legate Denpir to the King of Nioj. Along with war news, the Legate reports that Archbishop Gudurius recommends an assault on Turai as soon as the Orcs are defeated. His reasoning being that the Niojans will be able to wrest control of the city from the depleted Turanian forces.'

'I've talked to the Archbishop. He didn't seem hostile towards Turai.'

'He would be unlikely to admit his hostility to you.'

'True. He was much more friendly than I anticipated, which did make me suspicious. Did you inform Lisutaris about the messages?'

'Yes. It's now vital that Bishop-General Ritari remains in control of the Niojan forces. Make sure your investigation doesn't weaken his position in any way.'

I don't like Hanama telling me how to do my job, though she's right.

'It would also be helpful if you could discredit the Archbishop.'

'Nothing I can do will discredit a Niojan Archbishop.'

'You already suspect him of being behind the murder of Captain Istaros.'

I shrug my shoulders. 'Even if I proved he was, the Niojans wouldn't pay any attention to a Turanian investigator.'

'They might,' says Hanama. 'King Lamachus is very strict in his prohibition of infighting between senior figures at his court. Even if the Archbishop was never prosecuted it would weaken his influence if he were found to have been attacking his colleagues.'

One again, Hanama is talking sense. I'm surprised by the conversation. With her suggestions of what's best for Turai, it almost sounds like the diminutive assassin has loyalty to the city. I've never suspected her of that before. The notion that she might have loyalty towards Turai makes me marginally more sympathetic towards her.

'One more piece of information, Captain Thraxas, concerning the fight which occurred in Elath between Captain Istaros and the

Archbishop's guards. The man who was killed was a priest named Osbaros. He was a senior figure in the Archbishop's retinue, and something of a favourite. Why the combat occurred is a mystery. If anyone has information, they're keeping it well guarded.'

'If this Osbaros was a favourite of the Archbishop's, it does make it more likely that he's taking revenge. Thanks for the information, Captain Hanama.' I pause. 'You know the Niojan investigator suspects you killed Legate Apiroi?'

'I've been suspected of killing a lot of people,' says Hanama, with a trace of cold humour that's rather untypical of her.

'If it's proved against you there will be trouble from Nioj.'

'I understood our Commander instructed you to deal with it.'

'She did. I'll do my best.'

Captain Hanama departs. Rinderan is waiting at the wagon. 'Captain Thraxas, I followed Pontifex Agrius, the Samsarinan priest. When he went out walking he spoke to the troops as he said, but he didn't do that for long. Gave them a few words of encouragement but he seemed in a hurry. So much so that it wasn't hard to avoid him seeing me. I followed him to the furthest edge of the Samsarinan encampment, close to the Simnians and Niojans, then he disappeared into a medical tent. There was a man stationed outside. I had the feeling he was there as a lookout.'

'What did you do?'

'I sneaked behind the tent and listened.'

I nod approvingly. 'Good work.'

'I don't think sickness or injury is the main business of that medical tent. At least, Pontifex Agrius wasn't sick or injured. He was buying dwa.'

'Dwa? Are you sure about that?'

'Quite sure. I could hear clearly. After he was gone, I would have investigated more but I couldn't risk being seen by the lookout, so I don't have any other evidence. But I'm certain I heard them discussing dwa.'

'Well done, Ensign Rinderan. This fits in with my suspicions. Was this medical tent anywhere near where Major Magranos was killed?'

'Very close. Does that have something to do with his death?'

'Dwa usually has something to do with deaths in the area.'

That's not my only suspicion. Makri was seen nearby. That's why Baron Vosanos suspects she killed Magranos, but I'm thinking revenge probably wasn't the reason Makri was in the vicinity of a dwa dealer. She's shown a troubling partiality for the drug on previous occasions, particularly during stressful times. It might explain her strange behaviour in the trench, though her animated behaviour didn't quite match the symptoms of a dwa addict. My thoughts are interrupted by the arrival of Anumaris. Unlike Rinderan and me, she's neat and tidy and still doesn't look anything like a soldier.

'Captain Thraxas.' Her voice sounds strained. 'Sareepa Lightning Strikes the Mountain asks me to inform you she will be here later with beer.'

'That's the best news I've had all day.'

Anumaris is staring at me in an odd manner. 'Did you really strike Ensign Makri in the face?'

'What?'

'I was shocked to hear it. War is stressful but there's no excuse for this.'

'Anumaris, be quiet. I did not strike Makri. Don't repeat such falsehoods again.'

'I heard you—'

'Whatever you heard was wrong. There was no violence.'

Anumaris looks mollified, to an extent. At this moment Droo bounds into view. 'I heard Thraxas stabbed Makri! What happened? Why did you do it?'

'I did not stab Makri! What's the matter with you all? Don't you know how these foolish rumours spread in wartime? Stop believing every ridiculous thing you hear.'

'It's not that ridiculous,' protests Droo. 'People say you were always fighting in Turai.'

'People should mind their own business. I have never struck Makri. I'm known for encouraging her various endeavours. Anumaris, when is Sareepa expected?'

'Any time. You should get ready.'

'Ready? I'm ready now.'

'You're filthy. You look like you've been crawling in mud.'

'I was in a trench beneath a dragon. How do you expect me to look?'

Anumaris raises her hand. I feel a brief warm glow.

'Was that a tidy up spell? Didn't you do that once before? Didn't I tell you not to do it again?' I pause. I do feel better. Looking down at my previous dirt-caked attire, I seem to be quite tidy. And clean. 'Maybe it wasn't such a bad idea. Although Lisutaris has forbidden all sorcery that's not directly for the war effort.'

'I can hide it,' says Anumaris. 'Make it look like it was for investigating.'

Anumaris Thunderbolt is not so bad I suppose. Surprisingly helpful at times. I'm about to thank her when I feel a hearty clap on my back, strong enough to send me forward a few inches.

'What's this I hear about you fighting a dragon?' cries Sareepa, laughing.

'Had to hold it off till Lisutaris got there.'

'What were you doing in the trench?'

'Encouraging Makri. She was sure her calculations would fail but I had faith in her. About this beer?'

Sareepa indicates the bag she's carrying. 'You're slipping, Thraxas. Time was you'd have hunted out your own beer.'

'People are better at hiding it these days. They know I'm coming. It's almost as if people have been spreading rumours.'

Daylight is beginning to fade. It's on my mind that I should be doing something about Makri. If she's really been taking dwa it's a serious matter. She needs a clear mind for her calculations. One mistake and she could kill us all. I shrug, mentally. She's probably going to kill us all anyway. Might as well be full of beer when it happens. If the Orcs start flooding through our encampment I'd as soon be intoxicated. So I forget about Makri and welcome Sareepa Lighting Strikes the Mountain into the wagon, with her bag of clinking beer bottles.

'You never have explained to me, Sareepa, how you went from the worst-behaved, unruliest, youngster at sorcery school to Head of the Sorcerers Guild in Mattesh? What happened? Was it a sudden conversion or did you just get fed up using your sorcery to steal klee from your professor's secret cabinet?'

Sareepa laughs. 'I never stopped stealing klee from his cabinet. Four years of study and he never knew it was me. But some other things changed. Not all of them good.' She pops the top off one of her bottles. I hold out the strong leather tankard I've been using during the campaign. Sareepa fills it up. I like Sareepa. I like anyone who brings me beer. 'I'm sorry I almost poisoned you to death at the Sorcerer's Assemblage. I shouldn't have done that.'

'Forget it,' says Sareepa. It turned out well enough in the end.'

Chapter Twenty-One

I wake up next morning on the floor, half covered by a blanket, in a wagon that smells of beer. Beside me, also partially covered by the blanket, is Sareepa. Is that the second time we've spent the night together, or the third? I can't quite remember.

'Captain Thraxas, are you in there?' It's Droo, shouting from outside the wagon. 'Makri's here and Commander Lisutaris wants to see you.' For a small Elf she has a loud voice. With the lack of tact I've come to expect, she sticks her head through the curtain. The young Elf sees Sareepa, grins, and withdraws from the wagon. 'Hey Makri? Do you really need Thraxas right now? Can it wait?'

'Why?'

'He's in there with Sareepa. Looks like there was a lot of beer involved. Maybe should leave them for a while.'

Makri's reply sounds cold. 'Our Commander requires his presence immediately.'

'OK.' Droo attempts to stick her head back into the wagon but by this time I'm in position to repel her, shoving her back through the curtain. 'I'll be out in a minute,' I grunt, and start getting dressed, which is difficult in the confined space, particularly as my clothes appear to be strewn around in a random manner, mostly under beer bottles. As I'm strapping on my sword, Sareepa opens her eyes.

'Morning,' she says.

'I've been summoned by our Commander.'

'Fine,' says Sareepa. She closes her eyes and goes back to sleep. The Matteshan sorcerers never seem to be involved in early morning activities. I envy them. Outside, Makri is waiting for me in her light Orcish armour. Like everything else in camp it's dusty and travel-worn, though she maintains it well enough. Better than I treat my own gear, probably.

'Lisutaris needs to see me? Why so early?'

'War does not wait on your convenience.' Makri doesn't seem in the greatest of moods. She's not really a morning person either. I follow her though the camp towards the command tent. As we approach, one of our Commander's young messengers races past us and enters the tent. By the time we reach there he's on his way out again, busy and enthusiastic as these messengers always are.

Makri turns to me. 'You stink of beer.'

We enter Lisutaris's command tent. Lisutaris sniffs the air. 'Captain Thraxas. You stink of beer.'

'So I've been informed. The early summons caught me by surprise.'

'Early summons or not, I've instructed you not to drink.'

'I believe the instruction was to drink less. Which I've been doing, thanks to the outrageous beer shortage.'

'Thraxas, if I didn't have so much on my plate at this moment I'd be down on you like a bad spell. I've already had two messages this morning, one from Legate Denpir and one from Bishop-General Ritari, and I didn't like the tone of either of them. Both are demanding an immediate answer to who killed Captain Istaros. Can we provide that?'

'Not yet. The evidence is pointing towards Archbishop Gudurius. Not him personally, but I think he was behind it.'

Lisutaris raises her eyebrows. 'Interesting. Tell me more.'

'Istaros got in a fight with the Archbishop's men in Elath. Killed one of his favourites. Now Istaros and the other members of the unit he was with are being killed off.'

Lisutaris becomes slightly less displeased. 'If Archbishop Gudurius is behind the murder of the King's nephew, that's good for us. Did Hanama inform you of his desire to attack Turai?'

'She did.'

'Anything that would make him fall out of favour with the King would be a help.' Lisutaris lights a thazis stick. 'This may all work out well after all. Can you find evidence against him?'

'Possibly. But the King of Nioj isn't going to prosecute his archbishop just because a Turanian investigator says he's guilty.'

'A prosecution won't be necessary. If we had evidence, I have enough diplomatic influence to make sure Archbishop Gudurius and Legate Denpir fall out of favour. Keep investigating.'

'Yes, Commander.'

Lisutaris finishes her thazis stick and lights another. Whatever efforts she may have made to cut down on the substance have fallen by the wayside. Her addiction is as bad as ever. 'Makri informs me that her new Elvish mathematician is a considerable help. Quick to learn, apparently. They might get us to the walls after all.' Lisutaris frowns, very deeply. 'When we do take the city back, I'm damned if I'll lose it to the Niojans. Keep me informed of progress, Captain Thraxas. Whatever happens, don't implicate Bishop-General Ritari in anything bad.'

'Yes, Commander.'

I leave Lisutaris's command tent and walk through the camp. I'm fed up walking through this camp. I've done a lot of it, to little effect. I frequently walked around Turai, investigating, but the city was full of taverns where a man could drink beer and ease his troubles. Here there are no taverns and precious little beer. A feeling of gloom envelops me as I realise how long it is since I've been in a decent tavern. Not since we left Samsarina, and it's not like their taverns were so great. Nothing like the Avenging Axe where I could rely on a hearty meal cooked by Tanrose every day, and one of Gurd's *happy guildsman* extra-large sized flagons of ale in front of a roaring fire with genial company, and Makri behind the bar, insulting customers and raking in the tips in her chainmail bikini. I wonder if those days will ever return? I have my doubts. Who knows if the Avenging Axe even exists any more? The city is full of Orcs. If they learned that the Avenging Axe was home to Thraxas, feared warrior and implacable defender of Turai, they'll have destroyed it out of spite. Damn those Orcs. My mood worsens. I've come to talk to Bishop-General Ritari but I have to wait outside his command tent while he confers with his officers. By the time I'm allowed access I've abandoned all thoughts of diplomacy.

'Bishop-General, I'd like some answers. Your secret defence unit - was Captain Istaros a member? Why was he in Elath and were there other members of your defence unit with him?'

Ritari is surprised by my questions but he's too experienced to panic in the face of hostile interrogation. He takes some moments to compose himself before answering. 'Captain Istaros was a member of that unit.'

'And Captain Taijenius? Who unfortunately committed suicide. Though his brother doesn't believe that and I don't think I do either.'

'The investigation seemed clear.'

'The investigation was worthless. He could have been murdered and it could have been covered up with sorcery. Wouldn't even need sorcery if the investigation was bad enough.'

The Bishop-General doesn't seem surprised by this. 'I know. I half suspected it myself. There was no proof.'

'What were they doing in Elath?'

'Captain Istaros was buying land.'

'Did he need your defence unit to help him?'

'They weren't there on official duties, Captain Thraxas. More as companions. The swordfighting tournament was taking place, many people are keen to visit Elath to see it.'

'True. But I'm finding it strange that your entire defence unit appeared in Elath at the same time.'

'They were companions, there to watch the tournament while Istaros made his land purchase. I don't see anything strange about that.'

'They got into a fight and a man was killed. That was strange.'

The Bishop-General takes this calmly. 'Yes. A regrettable incident. But these things will happen, I suppose, when young men gather in numbers at a swordfighting tournament. Excitement gets out of hand, a few harsh words can lead to trouble...'

'You're making it sound all very innocent. The fact is, they killed one of Archbishop Gudurius's men and then fled Samsarina. That was more than a little quarrel. Care to tell me what it was about?'

'I never learned the nature of the argument. I regretted it of course, and sent my condolences to the Archbishop.'

'How did he take that?'

'Very civilly.'

I raise my eyebrows. 'Really? So you don't think he's out for revenge?'

'What makes you think that?'

'Your dead employees. Istaros and Taijenius.'

Ritari is derisive. 'Are you inferring the Archbishop is behind their deaths? Hardly likely. Nioj's senior cleric does not go around assassinating people, whatever may happen in other nations. Captain Thraxas, I've given you a lot of my time. I really must bring this to an end now.'

Before he throws me out, I manage one more question. 'How many other members of this defence unit are there?'

'Just one, in this encampment. Ensign Valerius. An excellent young soldier.'

'I'll need to talk to him.'

'Of course. I told you we would cooperate with your investigation.' With that, Ritari ushers me out. An aide outside the tent informs me as to the location of Ensign Valerius. I should visit him immediately. Though I would like some beer. I walk south, debating which to do first - talk to Valerius or locate beer. Preoccupied, I almost bump into Anumaris. She tells me she's been looking for me. She's keen to carry on our investigation as we might not have much time left to reach a conclusion. I tell her about my interview with Bishop-General Ritari.

'So now I have to interview this Ensign Valerius. Last member of Ritari's special defence unit in the camp.'

'I'll accompany you.'

'If you want. But I'm looking for beer first.'

'I suppose a detour to find beer wouldn't hurt,' says Anumaris.

I come to an abrupt halt. 'Pardon?'

The young sorcerer looks apologetic. 'I think I've been too harsh on the subject. I don't suppose Lisutaris meant to forbid you from drinking at all. I'm sorry if I've gone on about it too much.'

It's a heartening speech. 'I'm pleased to hear it. In that case, follow me to the Simnian encampment. I know what you're thinking - what business could an honest Turanian have with that foul bunch–'

'I have nothing against Simnians.'

'–but the fact is, war sometimes calls for desperate measures, even if it means collaborating with these uncivilised swine. If any of them become aggressive, fire a few spells at them, that'll shut them up.

We head off in the direction of the Simnian encampment. I'm searching for Calbeshi, their quartermaster. I find him lounging on a stool with his back against a wagon full of crates marked *salted beef*. Calbeshi's a large man, bald, ugly, and getting flabbier by the day. I've had the misfortune to know him for a long time and greet him accordingly. 'No surprise to find you lounging around like the lazy Simnian dog you are while others do the work.'

'It that Thraxas? I heard your fat hide got squashed by a dragon. Sorry to see it isn't true.'

'Takes more than a dragon to defeat a Turanian warrior.'

'A dragon probably couldn't fit you in its mouth. Are you here begging for beer again, you useless excuse for a soldier?'

'Of course. You think I'd wander into your damned Simnian pit for any other reason?'

'Our beer is for Simnian heroes.'

'There never were many of them.'

'We'll roll over your little city-state one of these days. If the Niojans don't destroy you first.'

Calbeshi leans down and reaches below the wagon from where he draws out a crate. 'You know there's a shortage? God knows why I'd give you any.'

'Because I saved your life twenty years ago in Mattesh.'

'You mean I saved your life. I can still remember what a pathetic soldier you were. I must have been feeling pity for you ever since.' Calbeshi tosses me a large bottle of beer, which I catch. 'Never bother me again.'

'Thanks for the beer. I'll be in the front lines, saving your life while you're hiding in your wagon.'

Calbeshi laughs. 'When you're fleeing, the Simnians might save you, if you're lucky.'

I stroll off, beer in hand. I snap the top off with a well-practiced manoeuvre and sip it as I walk.

'That seemed to go well,' says Anumaris.

'It's all a matter of knowing how to talk to them. Skills I've learned from years of soldiering and investigating. Although–' I pause. '–my skills didn't do me much good when I was talking to Bishop-General Ritari. He claimed to know almost nothing.

Everything was a mystery to him. Even when I gave him the opportunity to blame everything on Archbishop Gudurius he didn't take it. You'd have thought he'd be keen on doing that. Get one over on his rival.'

'Perhaps what Captain Hanama told us was true. Important Niojans don't like to be seen to be rivalling each other. Their King doesn't like it.'

'That could account for it. It might suit him better if any accusations came from me, rather that him. Keeping his hands clean, as it were.'

'Do you think Archbishop Gudurius really is behind the murders?'

'I'm almost certain of it. Nothing else seems to fit. Though it's all been professionally done. Not much evidence left.'

'What happens if we can't find proof?' wonders Anumaris.

'I don't know. I'm used to dealing with small-time crooks in Turai. This affair - Kings, generals, archbishops - I'm in over my head.'

'I don't think that's true. You've done well so far.'

'You think so?'

'Of course. Look how much we know now. You're a good investigator.'

I'm surprised at her support. I appreciate it. We walk through the Niojan lines, following directions towards Ensign Valerius's tent. When we draw near we find a crowd gathered outside. I force my way through. Beside the tent Valerius is lying dead with an arrow in his back.

I sigh, quite loudly. 'Anumaris, use whatever magic you have to see if you can find anything relevant. I'll examine the body.'

Chapter Twenty-Two

I waken in the wagon with Sareepa. For a moment I enjoy the feeling of the warmth of her body next to mine. Then I realise I've woken up puzzling about the case. It's irritating. Another murder. Ensign Valerius, dead. The combined talents of Anumaris and myself found nothing. No clues that could give us any sort of lead. Even though we were there within minutes of the death, there was no evidence. Just a lot of people milling around, none of whom had seen anything or knew anything. If I hadn't gone to visit Calbeshi for beer, I might have arrived at Valerius's tent in time to prevent him from being killed. I'm surprised Anumaris didn't point it out to me. Now I think about it, Anumaris was unusually civil. Didn't mind me wandering off to find beer. Told me I was a good investigator. What's got into her? My thoughts are interrupted by Hanama, who somehow appears next to me in the darkness. It's startling and annoying.

'Hanama?' I hiss. 'What the hell are you doing?'

For the only time since I've known her, the diminutive assassin looks embarrassed. 'I have news,' she whispers. 'I thought you'd be alone.'

'Damn you and all assassins.' I say this with feeling, though still keeping my voice down so as not to wake Sareepa. I rise rapidly, wrap my cloak around me and hustle Hanama out of the wagon. Outside it's dark, one moon hanging low in the east and a host of stars visible in the night sky. It's an hour before dawn, and cold.

'How dare you break into my wagon!'

'I did not expect you to be in the company of Sareepa!' Accidentally stumbling upon me and Sareepa has disconcerted her.

'Even if I was alone I don't want people sneaking up on me in the middle of the night.'

'My unit has identified an assassin in the Niojan ranks. His true name is unknown but when I last encountered him he was going by the name of Scletin.'

'I thought the Niojans didn't have an Assassins Guild?'

'They don't. However they do have assassins. Scletin learned his trade in Samsarina. Other than that, we don't know much about him. I thought you'd want to know. A skilled assassin in the Niojan ranks might explain why the recent murders have yielded few clues.'

'Has he just arrived?'

'Uncertain. He may have been keeping out of sight. He could have been assisted by sorcery.'

'How did you find him?'

'Through Megleth.'

Megleth is an Elf who's working in Hanama's unit. Hanama claims she can't be fooled by sorcery. I'm dubious about that. Nonetheless, I'm interested to learn that the Niojans have an assassin skulking in their camp. It's useful information, and not the only useful information Hanama has provided. I attempt to say something helpful in return. 'The Niojans still suspect you of killing Legate Apiroi. I haven't found a way to dissuade them but I'll keep trying.'

Hanama doesn't react. I don't think she's capable of expressing gratitude. She turns and leaves. I watch after her for a moment, then shiver in the cold air. Faint signs of dawn are appearing on the horizon. I climb back into the wagon. Sareepa stirs, and wakens. 'Who was that?'

'Captain Hanama.'

'What did she want?'

'Nothing important.'

I lie down next to Sareepa and we both go back to sleep. Commander Lisutaris has called a meeting of her senior officers tomorrow to which I'm invited, for some reason. I should be properly rested. For the next few hours, no alarms sound, no dragons attack, and I'm undisturbed. As a consequence I'm unusually relaxed as I stroll towards the command tent shortly before noon. I join in with the military men who've been summoned by Lisutaris. There's General Hemistos, infantry commander, in his green Samsarinan uniform; the black-clad Bishop-General Ritari our cavalry commander; and Lord Kalith-ar-Yil, leader of the Elvish contingent. Walking beside them is General Morgias, the senior Simnian officer, who wears a dull red tunic with some fancy black piping denoting his rank, and Admiral

Arith, head of the navy. Yesterday the camp was resupplied from the flotilla which shadowed us along the coast. Here, near the harbour of Turai, we're close enough for them to support us. Close enough for the ships to take off survivors if we suffer catastrophic defeat, though no one is mentioning that.

Inside the command tent various others are waiting. Captain Hanama, and senior sorcerers from different nations - Coranius, Tirini, Sareepa, Gorsoman, Charius the Samsarinan, Irith Victorious from Juval, and some others I don't know. Also present is Major Erisimus, the Simnian in charge of digging the trench. There's not much talking going on and the assembly falls silent as Lisutaris addresses us. 'The trench has almost reached Turai. Within twenty-four hours we'll be in a position to undermine the west wall and bring it down. When that happens our assault troop of sorcerers and marines will lead our troops into the city. All of you know the tasks you've been given and I expect those tasks to be carried out to efficiently. By this time tomorrow we'll be in control of Turai with the Orcs either dead or fleeing east.'

It's a short, confident speech, greeted mostly by expressions of approval. I notice one or two doubtful faces, one of those being the Niojan, Legate Denpir. 'Commander,' says the Legate. 'The trench has been advancing, protected by sorcery. We're given to understand that directing this sorcery requires some very advanced mathematical formulas.'

'That's correct.'

'Our chief mathematician, Arichdamis, unfortunately passed away.'

'A sad loss,' says Lisutaris. 'However, not fatal to our plan. His assistant, Lezunda Blue Glow, has coped admirably.'

'Really?' A faint sneer appears on the legate's face. 'I've heard from a reliable source that Lezunda Blue Glow has no more idea of mathematics than I do. The calculations are being performed by the Orcish woman you employ as your bodyguard.'

Many surprised glances are directed in the direction of Makri, currently standing behind Lisutaris, looking uncomfortable.

'Is this true?' demands the Legate. 'Are we expected to commit troops into battle under the directions of a female Orc?'

Lisutaris's eyes narrow. She draws herself up. If surprised by the Legate's accusations she recovers quickly. 'Firstly, Legate. Ensign Makri is not an Orc. She has Orcish blood, as has never been denied, but has served this army and the city of Turai with great bravery. Secondly, she is not in control of the calculations. Lezunda is, with the assistance of the Avulan Elf Sorelin. Ensign Makri has merely been helping check the figures.'

All eyes are still on Makri. She's agitated. Not surprising. She hates being called an Orc. Were we anywhere else she'd have attacked Legate Denpir by now, but here, as Lisutaris's bodyguard, she's on her best behaviour. Makri's best behaviour isn't that great, now I consider it. I take a step towards her, to intercept if she suddenly flies at the Legate.

'I will not allow us to be distracted by foolish rumours.' Lisutaris speaks forcibly but the allegation from the Niojan Legate is so troubling that she doesn't manage to bring the awkward situation to an end. General Morgias, the Simnian commander, speaks up. 'Simnian troops would hesitate to attack the walls under these circumstances, Commander. Our senior sorcerer, Gorsoman, has already expressed doubts about the plan. Were it known that the sorcery depends on an…on your bodyguard, there would reluctance to follow it.'

Makri looks increasingly uncomfortable. I notice her brow is glistening. Lisutaris raises her voice. Not too much, not feeling it politic to shout at her commanders, but enough to show she's angry. 'Enough of this. The calculations as performed by Lezunda Blue Glow and Sorelin have proved to be accurate. Sorcery has flowed along the trench and the Orcs have not been able to penetrate it. That alone should give you confidence. The plan will proceed as stated. By tomorrow we'll be ready to attack. See that your troops are well-prepared. Dismissed.'

Everyone else leaves the tent. I remain. Lisutaris isn't keen on my continuing company. 'That will be all, Captain Thraxas.'

'Busy?'

'Very busy. Leave now.'

'I'd rather stay. I'm curious as to which particular substance you've been giving to my old companion Makri.'

Lisutaris's eyes flash. 'What do you mean by that?'

'Makri's been acting strangely. Over-confident at times, paranoid at other times. And agitated, like now.'

'No wonder she's agitated! A plague on Legate Denpir and his rumours.'

'I've seen Makri fight a dragon and she wasn't agitated. Not like this. Look, she can hardly stand still. Her brow is dripping with sweat. That's not normal. What have you been giving her?'

'Damn you Thraxas, get out of my tent.'

'From Makri's visits to a dwa dealer and your own supplies of extremely strong thazis, I'm guessing you've made some concoction to keep her going, boost her capacity for work and bolster her confidence.'

'That is a ridiculous accusation, made with no evidence whatsoever!'

'But it's true, isn't it?'

'Certainly not,' cries Lisutaris. 'Makri is perfectly healthy.'

Makri collapses and lies face down on the floor.

Lisutaris looks at her prone body. 'It's probably just the stress.'

'Dammit, Lisutaris, what have you been giving her?'

'Nothing of any consequence! Merely a few drops of turix.'

'Turix? What's that?' By this time I'm kneeling by Makri's side. Her forehead is unnaturally warm and her pulse is low. When I look up Lisutaris is unlocking a metal box from which she produces a small book, an ancient-looking tome bound in black leather.

'*The Finely Honed Specific Death Spells of Julia the Bad*?' I'm incredulous. 'Julia the Bad? You've been dosing Makri with poison made by the most notorious sorcerer in history?'

'Turix is not poison. It's simply a potion used by experienced Turanian sorcerers to assist us in difficult times.'

'Does it include dwa and enhanced thazis?'

'The ingredients are secret,' says Lisutaris, stiffly.

I practically explode. 'What's the matter with Turanian sorcerers? Do you all have to be doped out your heads before you can function?'

'We've successfully protected the city for a long time,' mutters Lisutaris. By now she's throwing together herbs summoned from the temporary wooden shelving set up at the side of the tent. They fly from the shelves into a beaker at the twitch of her fingers. Making a potion is not something she'd normally do in company. I've never seen her do it before. The herbs are mixed in seconds. Lisutaris glances at Julia the Bad's spell book, then adds yellow liquid to the concoction, which she mixes by moving her finger in the air, having no need for anything as mundane as a spoon.

'You could have killed Makri, giving her this stuff.'

'Don't exaggerate, Thraxas. It's perfectly safe.'

'Then why is Makri lying on the floor?'

'I may possibly have given her a fraction too much. Understandable. It's been a tremendous help to her. This will bring her back to normal.'

Lisutaris kneels beside Makri and helps her to sip from the beaker. From the experienced way Lisutaris does this, I'm guessing it's not the first time she's assisted some unfortunate soul who's overdosed on the substance. Makri swiftly begins to return to normal. I'm relieved but it doesn't improve my mood.

'Does every Turanian sorcerer use this *turix*?'

'Only the most senior.'

'I've never heard of it.'

'Of course you haven't. It's one of our secrets.'

'So you're all full of dwa, thazis and foul herbs as instructed by Julia the Bad?'

Lisutaris shrugs. 'No need to make it sound so dramatic. We have a war to fight. Senior sorcerers are under great duress. You can't keep repelling dragons without a little extra support.'

'I think you can! Whatever happened to sorcerers in Turai? Used to be they just got drunk like everyone else. When did you all become so degenerate?'

Lisutaris helps Makri to a chair. She's left Julia the Bad's small book on the table. It's a rare item, not one I thought I'd ever see. The notorious Julia the Bad ended her stint as Head of the Sorcerers Guild with such an evil reputation that her legacy has mostly been erased, and her spells made taboo and forgotten. Or so

I thought, anyway. Naïve of me. The Turanian Sorcerers Guild obviously didn't intend discarding anything that might come in useful. Back in Turai, Lisutaris owned a very extensive collection of spells and spellbooks, one of the largest collections in the world. It's telling that she carries this one around with her.

I glance inside. The language is archaic, but legible. "Spell for killing father-in-law in autumn." "Spell for killing father-in-law in winter." I wonder what she had against her father-in-law. "Spell for killing father in law in Spring." Presumably he never made it to summer. "Spell for afflicting King's treasurer with painful injury if he dares question the finances of the Sorcerers Guild." "Spell for punishing a lover who has been proved to be visiting a brothel in Kushni after lying about his whereabouts." I shake my head. She obviously wasn't one to ignore an insult. Many of the spells are oddly specific. "Spell for killing dog that barks at night." "Spell for killing man wearing silver buckle." "Spell for killing half-brother." "Spell for killing woman who sews with golden thread in the morning."

'Did Julia the Bad actually use these?'

'Probably. There were a lot people she didn't like.'

At the back of the book are various miscellaneous spells, more general in scope. Several of them are of an offensive nature, for use against dragons, snakes and other beasts, and some for killing people directly. Then there are some recipes, including the one for turix, and an antidote in case too much was taken. Makri, now ingesting this antidote, stands up quite abruptly.

'Time to get back to work. I have mathematics to do.'

I tell her to sit down again. 'You should rest a while. Don't bother pretending you haven't been taking illicit substances.'

Makri glares at me angrily, but doesn't reply. I turn to Lisutaris. 'You shouldn't give this stuff to Makri.'

'I do whatever needs to be done.'

'I'm sick of you doing whatever needs to be done.'

'Fortunately, your opinion doesn't matter.'

I leave the tent, annoyed at everything. Outside it's very warm. The temperature is rising rapidly. Summer in Turai is hot as Orcish hell. If we take the city back we'll be rebuilding under the burning sun. Halfway towards my unit, I stop, pause, and think. I sit down on an empty wooden box, discarded by our supplies unit. I'm hot. I wonder why I didn't notice that before. Under my feet are the remains of several small flowers, trampled by the arrival of the army. We must have left a trail of crushed plants and flowers all the way from Samsarina to Turai, nature destroyed by our passing; rivers fouled, birds and animals fleeing. Overhead the skies are clear of birds. Normally, this close to Turai, you'd see some sign of stalls, the small black birds that infest the city, flying from rooftop to rooftop, ledge to ledge, singing shrilly to one another. The dragons have cleared them from the skies. I wonder if they're still lurking in the city. Maybe the Orcs have got rid of them. I doubt it: we never could. Above me I can see the faint glow of the sorcerous shield, now ever-present. I'm sick of living under a magical blanket. I'm sick of everything. I'm annoyed that Lisutaris would give a substance containing dwa and enhanced thazis to Makri, knowing quite well that Makri has in the past demonstrated a weakness for such things. Lisutaris doesn't care. I've been annoyed at her ever since she ordered Hanama to kill Legate Apiroi. Apparently being Head of the Sorcerers Guild has no ethical requirement. I think about things a little more. I hear a group of young Elvish soldiers laughing and that annoys me too. When I find myself being annoyed at the crushed flowers at my feet, I realise it's time to stop sitting around in a bad mood and go and do something. It's a short distance to my wagon. Sitting around are Anumaris, Droo and Rinderan. 'Droo, Rinderan, leave us. I need to talk to Anumaris in private.'

Droo and Rinderan look puzzled but leave without comment. I sit down on another old wooden box. It creaks under my weight. I haven't had a comfortable chair since I was chased out of Turai. 'Storm Class Sorcerer Anumaris, I'm annoyed. I'm annoyed at the heat and I'll be more annoyed when it gets hotter. I'm annoyed at the flowers we've crushed. I'm annoyed that young Elves are laughing. Mostly I'm annoyed at Lisutaris and you.'

'Why?'

'For misleading me, lying to me, hindering me and helping a murderer escape justice. Helping a murderer commit murder, possibly.'

Anumaris looks startled. Or pretends to look startled, I can't tell.

'What are you talking about?'

'You complimented me on my investigating prowess. I should have realised right away how suspicious that was. As suspicious as you telling me it was fine to go off hunting for beer. I've been on the wrong tack all along, and you encouraged me. At the behest of Lisutaris, no doubt.'

'You're not making sense, Captain Thraxas.'

'Really? Here's some things that don't make sense. Lisutaris claiming the Archbishop Gudurius was once in Turai, and was involved in the murder of his bishop. Gudurius has never been in Tura. I checked. The bishop in question is still alive and healthy. I doubt very much whether Hanama ever intercepted messages from Archbishop Gudurius to King Lamachus, recommending an attack on Turai, though Hanama's too loyal to Lisutaris to ever admit that. These were just ways of persuading me that Gudurius was behind Captain Istaros's murder. He wasn't. Captain Istaros wasn't in Elath innocently buying land either. He was sent there by Bishop-General Ritari to assassinate the Archbishop.'

'Doesn't that make it more likely the Archbishop would kill him? He'd want revenge.'

'He might. But the Niojan Archbishop is an experienced politician. He's not foolish enough to go around murdering people in the Niojan army while they're on campaign. Unlike Ritari, who is. Bishop-General Ritari is not an experienced politician. Something of a blunderer, in fact. He's been frantic to cover up his attempt to assassinate Gudurius ever since it failed. He knows how badly it would go for him if the King learned of it. Which is why he brought in his own assassin to get rid of Istaros and the other members of his own defence unit. Very cold-hearted. Though no more cold-hearted than Lisutaris, I suppose, who's been supporting him all along.'

'Lisutaris would not help Ritari murder his own men!'

'Maybe not, but she wouldn't go out her way to stop him either. Did you know Ensign Valerius was going to be killed? Is that why you didn't mind me going on a jaunt to find beer? Did Lisutaris send you to make sure I didn't get in the way?'

'That's preposterous,' says Anumaris. 'And none of this is true.'

'It's as close to the truth as I'll get. Lisutaris is an ally of Ritari. She's not going to let him be implicated in this, no matter how guilty he is.'

'Commander Lisutaris would only act in the best interests of the city.'

'Your opinion is noted. Now pack your bag and leave. I'm dismissing you from my security unit.'

'You can't dismiss me. Lisutaris placed me here.'

'Get your things and go. If you don't I'll pick you up and throw you over the wagon. Go back to Lisutaris and tell her I've finished the investigation.'

Anumaris draws herself up. Her eyes flash with anger. For a moment I think she might be about to use a spell. She turns on her heels without another word and strides swiftly towards her tent where she starts throwing her belongings into a bag. I look around, hoping there might be a bottle of beer in sight. There isn't.

'Eh...Captain Thraxas.' Rinderan approaches. 'Was all that really true?'

'Yes. Most of it anyway.'

'Is there evidence?'

'No.'

'Then how–?'

'I sat on a box and thought about things that were annoying me. Droo, do you have any beer?'

'No. I have wine.'

I take the bottle of wine from Droo. I'm drinking it as I leave the wagon, walking through the encampment to the Niojan position. I find Major Stranachus in front of his tent, on his own. 'You seem like a decent man. By Niojan standards anyway. Not that that's saying much.'

Major Stranachus raises his eyebrows. 'Good day to you too.'

'I'm here to give you some advice. Your investigation into Captain Istaros's death. Don't carry one with it. Let it go away. If anyone pushes you, just tell them you couldn't find any evidence.'

'Why would I do that?'

'Because if you carry on with it you'll probably end up dead.'

The Major rises rapidly and gets himself in front of me. 'Would you like to elaborate on that, Captain Thraxas?'

'Not much. I'll tell you two things, you can believe them or not. Someone tried to assassinate Archbishop Gudurius in Elath. One of his rivals.'

'His rivals? You mean Bishop-General Ritari?'

'I wouldn't like to give you a name. Second fact - Bishop-General Ritari now has an assassin in camp, working for him. He's been tidying up the loose ends.'

The Niojan investigator stares at me for some seconds. 'You expect me to believe you're giving me this information for the good of my health?'

I shrug. 'That's up to you.'

'It doesn't sound convincing.'

'Then carry on investigating. You can say hello to the Bishop-General's assassin when he calls.'

'If you think this will dissuade me from investigating the death of Legate Apiroi, you're mistaken. I know Captain Hanama killed him.'

'And I know the most powerful sorcerer in the west isn't going to let anything happen about that. Legate Apiroi was another rival of the Bishop-General's. Anyone who wants to stay healthy would do well to keep on his good side.'

'Are you claiming the Samsarinan Magranos was killed for the same reason?'

'I don't know why he was killed. Maybe he got too close to a dwa deal. Or possibly he witnessed something he shouldn't have.'

'Or possibly your friend Makri didn't like him.'

'Makri didn't kill him.'

'The Samsarinans think she did.'

'They have no evidence to support that.'

'Evidence?' The major laughs. 'You couldn't prove anything you've just suggested. Yet I'm supposed to take your word for it. Sounds to me like you're adjusting the facts to suit whatever your Commander wants to be true. Protect your friend Makri. Protect the assassin Hanama. Secretly blame Bishop General Ritari but keep his name out of it because you don't want to offend him.'

I'm not inclined to argue. 'Just accept we live in a world where powerful people do things we can't do anything about. There's no point getting involved too closely.'

'That's what investigators do.'

'Well, it's up to you.' I turn and leave. I'd rather Major Stranachus didn't end up dead. I walk back through the camp. The temperature seems to be rising by the minute. 'Hot as Orcish hell,' I mutter. I realise I'm still carrying Droo's wine. I probably cut a comical figure, talking to Major Stranachus. I don't care. I'm fed up with everything. Fed up with the war, the heat, the trench and the shortage of beer. Fed up with Lisutaris and Bishop-General Ritari pretending to care about who killed Captain Istaros. Fed up with Makri and her drugs and her mathematics. Fed up with Anumaris hindering me and reporting my every move to Lisutaris.

At the wagon I find Sareepa Lightning Strikes the Mountain waiting for me with a bag full of beer and her hair loose around her shoulders.

'You're the only thing in the world I'm not fed up with.'

Sareepa smiles. 'Are you talking to me or the beer?'

'Both of you.'

Chapter Twenty-Three

Sareepa wakes unusually early. I open my eyes to find her getting dressed. 'Did the alarm sound?'

'No. I have to report early. Commander thinks we'll be attacking soon.'

Our trench has almost reached the walls. Later today we'll likely be in action. Sareepa seems good humoured at the prospect. She's a powerful, experienced sorcerer, confident of her abilities in battle. 'When we've taken Turai I expect you to show me all the best places.'

'I live in an old tavern.'

'Sounds fine. We had some good times in old taverns.'

Sareepa slips out of the wagon. I get dressed. I'm not as good humoured about the prospect of battle as Sareepa though I'm not particularly worried. I've been to war many times. So far I've been fortunate. My luck will give out sometime; I've always known I'll die fighting the Orcs. If it happens today it's probably overdue. I wonder what the Orcs have planned. Prince Amrag and Deeziz the Unseen are not going to let us just stroll into the city, no matter how well our sorcerers are protecting the trench.

Makri clambers into the wagon with a scroll in her hand and a worried expression on her face. She's left the top button of her Orcish tunic unbuttoned, as if she dressed in a hurry. 'Thraxas, is this all a bad idea? Is it a terrible plan of attack?'

'Are you full of powerful, illegal drugs?'

'No, Lisutaris reduced the dose. I hardly notice the effect. Is our attack plan really bad? That Simnian sorcerer keeps calling it a bad plan.'

'I wouldn't say so. Undermining a city's walls used to be a standard siege tactic. It was successful, cities were taken that way. It only fell into disuse because sorcery became so powerful. Now we can protect our engineers, it's a decent plan.'

'Were there alternatives?'

'I didn't see any better. If we'd surrounded the city for a long siege, more Orcish forces might arrive from the east. As for storming the walls, we might lose half the army.'

'What about siege engines?'

'The west doesn't have a great supply of them anymore. The Orcs' sorcery would hold us off.'

I hunt around for beer. There isn't any. Sareepa and I must have finished it all off last night. 'Is there any reason for these questions?'

Makri shrugs. 'Not really. I expect the trench is going to fail because my calculations won't be right and we're all going to be killed. But at least it wasn't such a bad idea to try it.'

'Your calculations can't be that bad. We've reached the walls.'

'Only because of Sorelin. He's a very smart Elf. So intelligent I almost don't mind the way he's disgusted by my Orcish presence. But the last part is the hardest. We had to calculate a path that went downwards, and became wider. So there's enough room to light a fire under the foundations. The mathematics were especially difficult. It went into Arichdamis's final new dimension. When we calculated it we found two different answers.'

'Which one was right?'

Makri screws up her face. 'There was no way of telling. Remember I told you there were some things that couldn't be checked once the final version was made?'

'Yes.'

'This is one of them. We just had to guess which one was right and hand the calculations over to Lisutaris. We can't even check it again.'

'What happens if you picked the wrong answer?'

'We might produce the largest explosion in human history.'

'I'll look forward to it.' My foot touches something hard and sharp. I reach under the blanket on the floor of the wagon and emerge with a fancy silver flask.

'Sareepa's flask.' I open it. 'Klee. The morning just got better.' I take a healthy mouthful.

'You're drinking klee before breakfast?'

'Only because there isn't any beer.'

I hand the flask to Makri. She shudders as the powerful spirit trickles down her throat.

'Makri, I have a suggestion you're not going to like.'

'Is it fleeing on a horse to the furthest west? You might be able to talk me into it.'

'No, it's not fleeing on a horse. Stop worrying you're going to kill the whole army, you've done fine so far. My suggestion concerns a spell by Julia the Bad. Have you heard of her?'

'Yes. Head of the Sorcerers Guild last century. Powerful by reputation, and of dubious morals.'

'Indeed. Well I noticed a spell–'

'But I'm not sure I believe the dubious morals bit,' adds Makri.

'What?'

'I suspect it's just a story put around by men who were jealous of her.'

'Everyone does say she was bad.'

'Everyone?' sniffs Makri. 'The only people to write about her were men, after she died. It's quite likely they deliberately traduced her reputation.'

'*Traduced*? Is that a word?'

'Yes. History is full of men traducing women's reputations. The Association of Gentlewomen finds it very annoying.'

'All right Makri, I take your point. But if we could put that to one side for the moment, I read a few of her spells. Some of them were very specific, directed at people who offended her. Palace treasurers and her father-in-law came off badly. There was a spell in her book called "*Incantation for mounting a ruinous attack on a treacherous half-brother.*"'

'What about it?'

'Prince Amrag is your half-brother.'

Makri shrinks back a few inches. 'So?'

'It might be something Lisutaris could use against him once we get inside the city.' I look expectantly towards Makri, who's silent for a moment.

'I don't want to do it,' she says, finally.

'You should consider it.'

'If Julia the Bad wrote it for her own half-brother, it probably only worked on him.'

'Lisutaris is as powerful as Julia ever was. There a good chance she could adapt it to attack your half-brother. Probably only need to take some blood from you or something like that. Nothing too alarming.'

'Taking blood is quite alarming! You know I can't tell anyone that I'm related to Amrag.'

'I know you don't want to. Lisutaris would keep your secret safe.'

Makri looks very unhappy. 'I don't want to do it.'

'Well, it's up to you. I think you should consider it.'

'You're not going to give me away to Lisutaris are you?'

'Of course not. Thraxas will never betray a friend. Besides, I detest Lisutaris for her duplicity and hope to end this campaign never having to speak to her again.'

'Captain Thraxas? Ensign Makri?' A youthful messenger sticks his head through the canvas. 'You're both required to report to Lisutaris immediately.'

I buckle on my sword as we leave the wagon. The camp is coming awake, with breakfast fires being lit all over. We walk towards the command tent.

'Well Thraxas,' says Makri. 'This is probably it. We're going into action. We might not have a chance to speak again. Any final words?'

'Nothing I can think of.'

'Nothing?'

'What were you expecting?'

'How about "*It's great to have known you, Makri. You've been a wonderful friend and a tremendous help in everything. If by chance your errant mathematics get us all killed, I won't hold it against you.*"'

'Dammit Makri, if you get us all killed I'll come back from the dead and kill you again.'

A small group of officers are waiting outside the command tent. Makri is waved though by the guards but I have to wait in line. I don't care. I have no desire to talk to Lisutaris. Everyone else here is a senior order receiving their final orders for the attack. I'm surprised to be summoned at all, in the circumstances. Anumaris will undoubtedly have informed Lisutaris of my conclusions about my investigation, not to mention my feelings about Lisutaris's part in it. I doubt our Commander is that keen on me at this moment.

I wonder if the Orcs know we're attacking today. Our sorcerers have put up so many defensive barriers I'd be surprised if they have advance information, but you never know. We've underestimated the power of Deeziz the Unseen before. I glance up at the sky, half expecting to see dragons but the sun is too bright and I can't make out anything. The temperature is rising by the hour. I start to feel annoyed, being made to stand here waiting to enter the command tent. Petty revenge by Lisutaris, it wouldn't surprise me. The woman has never been suited for the role of War Leader. 'Turai would be nowhere without me,' I grumble, unfortunately saying it louder than I intended, possibly due to the klee I had for breakfast. The officers standing next to me give me something of a condescending look. Let them. I didn't see them standing on the walls fighting Orcs last time they attacked. I take out Sareepa's silver flask and sip more klee. Right then I'm summoned into the command tent and am still fumbling to put the flask away as I enter. Lisutaris notices but doesn't comment. She regards me in silence for a few moments before starting off in a neutral tone. 'Captain Thraxas. I've modified our plan of attack. The undermining of the walls will continue as planned but I will personally be leading our forces into the city.'

'I don't recommend that, Commander.'

Lisutaris smiles, quite grimly. 'Neither does Ensign Makri. Nonetheless, it's happening. My sorcerers have been trying to track the movements of the Orcish Sorcerers Guild. Difficult task, but we've made progress. As far as we can tell, Deeziz the Unseen has positioned herself and her strongest sorcerers right behind our point of entry. They'll try to prevent the wall coming down. If it does come down, we'll be faced by the most powerful group of hostile sorcerers ever assembled in one place. Consequently—' Lisutaris swiftly produces and lights a thazis stick '—I'll be leading our strongest sorcerers into the city at the head of our troops. We'll be accompanied by a unit from the Sorcerers Auxiliary Regiment.'

I nod my head. 'It makes sense, I suppose. I'm coming too.'

'As my security chief, you're not obliged to accompany the first wave.'

'I'm coming with you.'

'Good. We will appreciate your company.' Our Commander pauses. 'I notice you've been spending time with Sareepa Lightning Strikes the Mountain.'

I'm surprised to hear Lisutaris mention this. 'I have, Commander.'

'You realise none of us may survive this attack?'

'Yes.'

'Have you actually said anything nice to her?'

'Pardon, Commander?'

'Have you said anything warm, endearing or any more pleasant than asking her to pass you the next bottle of beer?'

'Probably not,' I admit.

'As I suspected. Well I suggest that you do, Thraxas. She's an old friend of mine and if we're all about to die I'd rather you sent her off with something better to remember than you guzzling beer.'

'I'll do my best.' I notice Makri is smiling. Next thing they'll be asking me to take her flowers.

'Anumaris Thunderbolt informs me you've reached some conclusions in your investigation into the death of Captain Istaros.'

'I have, Commander.'

'Apparently Bishop-General Ritari is responsible for everything. Sent his men to assassinate Archbishop Gudurius, and when that failed, sent his assassin to kill his own men so no one would find out about it. Is that accurate?'

'Yes.'

'Do you have proof of any of this?'

'No. I'm sure that's what happened but there's no proof.'

'Correct me if I'm wrong - I do suffer from the occasional memory lapse - but did I not instruct you to manage things so that Bishop-General Ritari didn't emerge from this affair looking bad?'

'Yes, but–'

'And now here you are, reporting that not only has the Bishop-General been involved in a plot to assassinate the Niojan Archbishop, he's attempted to cover it up by hiring assassins to kill his own men! Behaviour so dishonourable that were it to become known, he'd be lucky to escape execution at the hands of King Lamachus!' Lisutaris glares at me. 'Well? What do you have to say?'

'I'd say you should stop pretending to be outraged because you suspected it all along. It's not my fault if the Bishop-General turns out to be a violent gangster. When I'm asked to investigate something I investigate it. Don't blame me if it doesn't go the way you want.'

'Why not? If you hadn't poked around in places you probably shouldn't have been poking around in, then none of this would be known.'

'You demanded I investigate!'

'I demanded you did something to keep the Niojans happy and make sure it didn't bother me.'

'Were you expecting me to just make something up and blame someone else?'

'Wasn't that obvious?'

By now I'm glaring too. I've had enough of this. 'I find out the truth, when I can. That's my job. If you don't like the results, that's your problem.'

'Kindly watch your tone, Captain Thraxas,' says Lisutaris, ominously.

'Don't tell me to watch my tone, Commander. Tell me, was Anumaris just spying for you? Or did she actively hinder my investigation?'

'Are you accusing me of interfering?'

'Probably. When Anumaris used a tidying spell on me it struck me that she was still using magic when you'd forbidden it to everyone else. Who knows what other ways she might have tampered with evidence. Really, Lisutaris, if you wanted to go around murdering Niojan Legates and covering up the crimes of Niojan generals why bother to involve me at all? You should just have asked Anumaris to magic it all better.'

'I've had just about enough of you, Thraxas,' growls Lisutaris, ominously.

Makri takes a step forward. 'Commander. Thraxas did as instructed. You can't blame him if he found out the truth.'

'Ensign Makri, I didn't ask for-'

'Furthermore, we owe Thraxas for saving us from the sack of Turai. Probably other things as well. Also, you invited Captain Thraxas to the command tent to inform him of your new attack formation, not to berate him about his investigating.'

By this time Lisutaris is quite startled. 'Really, Ensign Makri? Is there anything else you'd like to lecture me about?'

'No, Commander. But I should tell you Prince Amrag is my half-brother. Thraxas says Julia the Bad had some spell that might be useful against him.'

Lisutaris's eyes widen in surprise. 'What? Are you serious? Why didn't you tell me this before?'

'I preferred to keep it secret, Commander. I didn't think it would be important.'

'You're Prince Amrag's half-brother? Of course that's important.' Lisutaris snaps her fingers and mutters a word, simultaneously causing a thazis stick to leap from one pocket of her cloak and Julia the Bad's spell book to appear from another. 'I'll need a little of your blood.'

'I knew it,' sighs Makri, and looks unhappy. I leave the tent. Outside it's hot as Orcish hell and troops are moving into position.

Chapter Twenty-Four

It's a struggle to reach Gurd's position. Soldiers aren't the only ones on the move. Now that the attack is imminent, non-combatants are beings sent to the rear. Cooks, tailors, metalsmiths, supply personnel and others make their way back towards the baggage train, some of them laden with goods, some hurrying as fast as they can. I'm hoping I can reach Gurd before Tanrose departs. I make it just in time, arriving as she's slinging a sack of cooking utensils over her shoulder. 'Tanrose, I need your help.'

Tanrose hands me a small parcel wrapped in a green cloth. She smiles. 'I was thinking of you, Thraxas. This is the last piece of cake I could make.'

I'm so surprised by this thoughtful action that for one of the very few times in my adult life, I'm almost moved to tears. I stand there like a fool, not knowing quite what to say. Beside us, Gurd senses my awkwardness. He claps me heartily on the shoulder.

'Best eat it quick, Thraxas, we'll be in action soon.'

Gurd's blow brings me back to my senses. I thank Tanrose profusely. 'The world needs more people like you Tanrose. I'll always be grateful for this piece of cake. However, that wasn't why I needed your help.'

'What's the matter?'

'Lisutaris told me I have to say something nice to Sareepa.'

Tanrose nods her head. 'I can see that would be a problem.'

'Do I really have to do it?'

'You probably should.'

'What were you planning on doing?' asks Gurd.

'Nothing. I thought we'd just go about our business as usual. Do I need some sort of farewell ceremony?'

'You're all in a lot of danger when you attack,' says Tanrose.

'No we're not,' protests Gurd.

Tanrose puts her hand on his arm and smiles. 'I know you are.' She looks at me. 'Gurd's been trying to convince me there's no danger. I'm not a fool, Gurd. I know how dangerous this attack is. So will Sareepa. She'll know none of you might survive it. So do the decent thing Thraxas, and tell her it was nice spending time with her, and you're glad you had the opportunity.'

I'm not liking the sound of this. *'It was nice spending time with her, and I'm glad I had the opportunity*? Does that fit the bill?'

'I think it will.'

By now officers are barking orders and troops are moving into formation. I thank Tanrose for the cake and leave quickly, allowing her a last few seconds alone with Gurd. I struggle through the throng towards my unit. Officers are shouting orders and dust is rising as troops move into position. On my way I run into Sareepa, who's leading her Matteshan sorcerers towards the front. I grab her arm, not very elegantly, and pull her to one side. I manage to blurt out the words as instructed by Tanrose. 'It was nice spending time with you. I'm glad I had the opportunity.'

Inside I'm writhing with embarrassment. It has to be one of the most inappropriate things ever said in wartime. I'm expecting Sareepa to either burst out in mocking laughter or, possibly, punch me. Neither happens. Instead she leans over, kisses me on the cheek and says 'Thanks. It was nice spending time with you too.'

Sareepa walks off, leading her sorcerers into action. I don't know if they heard the exchange or not. When I reach my unit's wagon, Anumaris is standing beside it.

'What are you doing back here?'

'Our Commander instructed me inform you that you have no authority to dismiss me.' Anumaris speaks quite defiantly. I don't intimidate her. She has the commander on her side.

Rinderan appears. 'Everyone ready?' The young sorcerer is nervous though he's trying not to show it. He's never been in action before. Like Anumaris, he's been roped into supporting the central assault force. Lisutaris will have sorcerers positioned throughout the army, maintaining the dragon shield as best they can, but she's recruited many of them to support her as she leads the troops through the trench. Already I can see many rainbow cloaks heading towards the command tent, some of them sorcerers from foreign guilds I don't recognise.

We pack our belongings in the wagon. Droo appears, yawning.

'What do we do with the wagon?' wonders Rinderan.

I shrug. 'Leave it here. We should have sent it back to the baggage train but I forgot to organise it.'

'It will be fine,' says Anumaris. 'Either we win then we can come back for it or we lose and we won't need it.' She's picked up the fatalism of the experienced soldiers around her. Either that or she's pretending she has. I suspect she's really as nervous as Rinderan.

'Droo, you're not coming with us.'

'Yes I am.'

'You're not. I need you to go back to your Elvish reconnaissance unit for the rest of the day.'

The young Elf looks upset. 'I want to join in the attack.'

'You can't. The wall breeching unit is for sorcerers and experienced warriors only. Teenage Elvish poets are not appropriate for the occasion.'

'But you're all going.'

'Droo, depart. I want you as far away as possible. Anumaris, Rinderan, prepare a spell for ejecting this Elf if she doesn't pack her things and leave immediately.'

Faced with this, Sendroo gives up. Very unhappily, she packs her few belongings and departs, grumbling all the while that it's not fair she's not allowed to join in the first attack. We watch her go.

'I'm glad you sent her away,' says Anumaris. 'I didn't want to see her killed.'

Neither did I. In truth, I don't regard either Anumaris or Rinderan as particularly suitable for the first assault, but their sorcerous power is needed. I pick up my shield.

'Time to go. Is anyone going to say "*Captain Thraxas, we saved you this beer specially for the occasion?*" And then produce beer?'

'No,' says Anumaris.'

'I really didn't think of it,' says Rinderan.

I shake my head. 'As a security unit, you're a disappointment.'

Trumpets sound. We walk forward. The confusion is lessening as the attack force takes shape. Lisutaris is standing near the trench with a group of powerful sorcerers. In front of her are the miners, ready to advance into the trench one last time. Wood has already been set near the breach, and they're carrying more. Flanking

Lisutaris are soldiers from the Sorcerers Auxiliary Regiment and flanking them are troops from Simnia and Samsarina. Behind are Niojans and an Elvish contingent, all ready to rush into the city when the wall comes down. Rinderan and Anumaris take their place with the sorcerers. I walk through the crowd to where Makri, in her full set of light Orcish armour, is standing beside Lisutaris. Lisutaris has a leather chestplate beneath her sorcerer's cloak, and, something I've never seen her wear before, leather breeches. On her feet are a pair of sturdy boots. It's the first time she's ever appeared in anything resembling military uniform. Many of the other sorcerers have adopted similar attire. Obviously they're not expecting it to be an easy matter, entering the city. A few feet away, Tirini Snake Smiter is wearing a dazzling rainbow cloak and pink and yellow shoes. As an outfit for storming a city, it could hardly be more unsuitable. You have to admire her, I suppose.

Coranius the Grinder appears, grim-faced as always, ready for action. As one of our most powerful sorcerers he'll be accompanying Lisutaris. Other powerful figures appear - Gorsoman, the senior Simnian sorcerer, Hendrith Seawave, the most experienced Elvish sorcerer in the army, and Harmon Half Elf, a Turanian who's just arrived from his duties with the navy. There's another senior sorcerer from Samsarina whose name I can't recall, a Niojan, and Sareepa, who looks calm, refreshed, and ready for action. I look back at the assembled troops. Attempting to hide behind the legs of a very large infantryman is Ensign Droo. The young Elf has apparently decided to disregard my orders and join the attack. Unwise, but it's too late to do anything about it now. Lisutaris's officers are having final words with her. When they withdraw, leaving Lisutaris flanked by her senior sorcerers, Makri steps directly to one side of her and I step to the other.

Gorsoman the Simnian raises his eyebrows. 'Are those two coming with us?'

'Yes,' replies Lisutaris.

'Shouldn't we sorcerers be closest to you?'

'I want them beside me. Captain Julius, order the diggers into the trench and signal the Auxiliary Regiment to advance. Sorcerers, follow me.'

Chapter Twenty-Five

I'm walking along the zigzag trench. It's in good repair, wooden panels on the walls and wooden slats beneath our feet. Our sorcery has protected it, exactly as planned. It bodes well for our attack but I'm worried. Lisutaris believes that Deeziz the Unseen is waiting for us directly ahead so she's withdrawn a lot of sorcerous power from the shield. It still arcs above us but there's less force protecting it. As we advance, a hail of missiles and projectiles rain down from the walls, pounding on the barrier. The ability of the shield to protect us is not my only worry. There's still the final results of Makri's calculations to be reckoned with. Major Erisimus and his miners have to complete the excavation under the walls, plant more wood, set it on fire and depart quickly. Our sorcery is still protecting them but if Makri's final calculations are wrong, anything could happen. Sorcery twisting the wrong way through some strange dimension resulting in a huge explosion, according to her. I'm not sure if that's a realistic assessment or just the result of paranoia brought on by the drugs Lisutaris has been feeding her.

Missiles rain from the sky. I turn a corner and keep going. For a moment my thoughts turn to Bishop-General Ritari and my investigation. What a waste of time that was. The entire efforts of my unit devoted to solving a case which nobody really wanted solving. Not Lisutaris or Ritari, certainly. Ritari was behind the deaths, Lisutaris knew it, and shamelessly concealed her knowledge, all the while putting pressure on me to implicate Archbishop Gudurius. I hope it all turns out to have been worthwhile. If Ritari is killed in the assault and Archbishop Gudurius ends up as the senior Niojan here, we're going to look extremely foolish. It strikes me I haven't seen Hanama for a while. Maybe Lisutaris has sent her to get rid of Gudurius under cover of battle. Nothing would surprise me. Except justice, I suppose. That would surprise me.

We come to a halt. Ahead of us the engineers have reached the wall. It's an uncomfortable wait. Projectiles pour onto the barrier overhead. We're close enough to the walls to see the assembled lines of Orcs atop them, hurtling missiles. Among them are sorcerers, now firing bolts of energy towards us. Lisutaris steps forward. 'As soon as the engineers light the fire I'm sending in an extra spell to make sure the foundations crumble. Captain Thraxas, would you mind standing directly in front of me? There may be some flying debris.'

Makri steps forward. 'I'm your bodyguard. I'll do it.'

I grab Makri by both shoulders and shove her backwards. 'Out of the way. This requires some bulk.'

Makri looks angry but as she steps forward, Lisutaris puts out her arm, blocking her path.

'Captain Thraxas is more suitable for this, Ensign Makri.'

Above us, Lisutaris's personal shield remains strong, a pale blue light protecting us against the intense barrage now coming from the walls. The noise is deafening as rocks, boulders, spears and arrows cascade down onto the sorcerous shielding. Major Erisimus appears at a run, his diggers behind him. 'Fire's lit, Commander.' He salutes swiftly and disappears back along the trench with his men, their task completed. The noise above us intensifies. Lisutaris strides forward. Further back along the trench our assault force crouches out of sight, ready to move the instant the wall collapses. We turn the final corner. Ahead of us a great gash has been hewn beneath the city wall. The gap has been filled with wood which is now burning. In normal circumstances this would be enough to bring down the wall but Lisutaris, assuming that the Orcish sorcerers will be working to prevent this, is now about to help matters along. She raises her arms and begins to chant.

'Commander! Dragon!'

We look up. Diving towards us is the largest dragon I've ever seen, so large it seems impossible it could fly. I can only imagine it's been kept a short distance away, in the Stadium Superbius perhaps, grown to stupendous size, and launched at us for its one and only mission, to crush the trench and everyone in it. Lisutaris is obliged to break off her incantation.

'Sareepa, Coranius, deal with it.'

Coranius the Grinder and Sareepa Lightning Strikes the Mountain both leap upwards till they stand above us on the ground at the edge of the trench. It's an impossible move for a normal person and must be some sorcerously enhanced manoeuvre worked out beforehand. As I watch they fire off spells at the monstrous beast hurtling towards us. Lisutaris starts to intone her own spell again. I look back at the walls. The flames seem to be dimming, which shouldn't happen. Lisutaris's eyes go purple as she concentrates her power. Though I never had any talent for sorcery I can generally sense its presence and at this moment I can sense it everywhere. I'm guessing Deeziz the Unseen is right behind that wall, attempting to extinguish the flames and keep Lisutaris out. Purple sparks are shooting from Lisutaris's fingertips. I step towards our Commander, ready to get in front of her as soon as she casts her spell. The noise above us is deafening. I try to focus my attention on Lisutaris but I can't resist a glance upwards and I get a glimpse of the most terrifying sight. The huge dragon, wounded and dripping blood from the sorcery of Coranius and Sareepa is still forcing its way downwards. It hits the trench at the same instant that Lisutaris fires her spell towards the walls. There's an explosion the like of which I've never experienced before. I'm hurled up in the air with dirt, masonry, bodies and bits of dragon battering me from every direction. When I come to ground I'm badly shaken. There's dust and smoke all around. I drag myself to my feet, choking in the dust. I'm still in the trench though there doesn't really seem to be a trench any more. It's been damaged beyond recognition, flattened by the impact of the dragon and the effect of Lisutaris's spell. And possibly, it strikes me, by something to do with Makri's calculations, because that was one hell of an explosion and I can't believe it was meant to happen.

Lisutaris is lying only a few feet away. She moans.

'Anything broken?'

'I don't think so.'

I help her to her feet. Makri emerges from the gloom, a sword in each hand. 'The walls are down,' she says.

I take a step forward. My foot catches on something. I look down. It's Coranius the Grinder. He's dead. I notice a familiar scrap of cloth next to him. Part of Sareepa's rainbow cloak. A few feet away lies Sareepa, her body in an awkward position. I kneel to check for a pulse. There's none. Sareepa is dead too. Behind us a trumpet sounds, the signal for our waiting troops to attack.

'Forward,' says Lisutaris.

I raise my shield and take the lead as we advance through the smouldering ruins of the walls. Then I walk into Turai, first man into the city.

The End

Martin Millar was born in Scotland and now lives in London. He is the author of such novels as Supercute Futures, Lonely Werewolf Girl and The Good Fairies of New York. He wrote the Thraxas series under the name of Martin Scott. Thraxas won the World Fantasy Award in 2000. As Martin Millar and as Martin Scott, he has been widely translated.

Printed in Great Britain
by Amazon